Starring
Arabelle

Starring Arabelle

Written by
Hillary Hall De Baun

Eerdmans Books for Young Readers
Grand Rapids, Michigan • Cambridge, U.K.

Text © 2012 Hillary Hall De Baun

Published 2012 by Eerdmans Books for Young Readers,
an imprint of Wm. B. Eerdmans Publishing Co.
2140 Oak Industrial Dr. NE, Grand Rapids, Michigan 49505
P.O. Box 163, Cambridge CB3 9PU U.K.

www.eerdmans.com/youngreaders

Manufactured at Worzalla, Stevens Point, Wisconsin, USA,
in July 2012; first printing

12 13 14 15 16 17 18   8 7 6 5 4 3 2 1

Library of Congress Cataloging-in-Publication Data

De Baun, Hillary Hall
Starring Arabelle / by Hillary Hall De Baun.
p. cm.
Summary: Arabelle starts high school with big dreams
which are soon dashed when she is discouraged from auditioning
for the school play and must volunteer at a nursing home,
but surprises await, both in the theater and at Heavenly Rest.
ISBN 978-0-8028-5398-1
[1. Theater — Fiction. 2. Old age — Fiction. 3. Nursing homes — Fiction.
4. High schools — Fiction. 5. Schools — Fiction.
6. Ukrainians — New York (State) — Fiction.
7. Student exchange programs — Fiction.
8. New York (State) — Fiction.]
I. Title.
PZ7.D339252Las 2012
[Fic] — dc23
2011042739

All excerpts from *You Can't Take It With You* are used by permission of
Anne Kaufman Schneider and Christopher Hart.

For Vincent, who never stopped believing
— *H. H. D. B.*

First Day

Deirdre Glendenning's flaming red hair matched the fire in her eyes. "Unhand me, you beast! I am not yours to be so ill-treated, nor will I ever be!" With the fury of one possessed, Deirdre lashed Squire Gunn across the face with her crop, flung herself onto his white mount, and galloped into the night . . .

Mrs. Archer poked her head out the front door. "Arabelle, why aren't you at the bus stop?"

Arabelle, anxious and queasy, hunched on the porch steps. "I want to finish the chapter, Mom. I'll flag the bus when it comes around the corner." She knew the book by heart, she had read it so many times.

"Please don't miss your ride. Today of all days."

"Mom! Don't worry." Arabelle turned the page. The novel's heroine, destined to become a famous actress, was charging across the moor, leaving behind forever her cruel and despised master.

Her stomach churning, Arabelle read the same page twice. Surely reading about someone who barely escapes with her life would take her mind off her first day of high school, where as a ninth grader she'd have to prove herself — not just once or twice, but over and over.

A sudden grinding of gears caught her attention.

"Wait! Stop!" She clattered down the porch steps, waving madly at the yellow bus with "James Madison Regional High School" painted on its side.

The bus slowed to a stop. The doors folded open. "Why weren't you at the bus stop?" the driver growled.

"Sorry." Arabelle dredged up a smile and stumbled to an empty seat as the bus started up with a lurch.

The dough-faced boy next to her grabbed Deirdre out of her hands. "What's this?" he wheezed, squinting at the dust jacket. *"Less Miserabulls?"*

"Give it here." Arabelle lunged for the book, but he held Deirdre over his head.

"Bet it's dirty."

"It is not!" Leaping, she seized her book and stuffed it in her backpack before someone else grabbed it.

She had no wish to be seen in public with a romance novel like *Ravished!* With its steamy cover of the legendary actress Deirdre Alexis Glendenning bursting her bodice, and some lovesick king or other kneeling at her feet, she'd be the butt of endless jokes. The dust jacket from her mother's book club edition of *Les Misérables* had offered the perfect disguise. If anyone challenged her, Arabelle knew all about Jean Valjean being a convict and wanting to improve the world. Thank God for *Les Miz*, which she had seen on cable.

The twenty-minute bus ride took forever. Arabelle gazed out the window and imagined how her day would start. First, she'd make friends with her locker neighbors.

"Hi," she'd say. "My name's Arabelle but everyone calls me Alex."

"How come?" they'd ask.

And she'd say, "My middle name's Alexis but I prefer Alex." She would not mention Deirdre.

"Awesome name," they'd tell her.

And she'd say, "I plan to audition for the school play."

And they'd say, "Good decision, Alex. Go for it!"

For the rest of the ride, Arabelle indulged her favorite daydream, in which she stopped being an average teenager from a boring town that no one had ever heard of and morphed into an exciting other person destined for greatness. The story never changed. Orphaned from birth, bound over to a troupe of actors, she overcame every obstacle on her grueling climb to stardom. Deirdre had achieved fame overnight, which Arabelle thought was grossly unfair. She could hardly hope for that, but starring in the school play would be the first giant step toward her goal. Her daydream always ended the same way: a final curtain call to a standing ovation.

Her bus, inching around the circular drive, was the last to unload in front of the sprawling, two-story brick and stucco building set down in what was once a cornfield between Albany, the state capital, and the small town of Grafton Green, where she had lived her entire life. Until this year she had walked to school.

Arabelle hesitated on the sidewalk, her smile permanently fixed as she strained for the sight of a friend from last year — someone to wave to, someone to walk and laugh up the steps with. A second later, she was pushed and elbowed through the arched front doors and deposited by the double-glass bulletin boards bearing locker assignments.

Arabelle finally located hers in the milling confusion of the hall. According to the alphabetical list, Jeff Anderson was on one side of her, Bonnie Atwood on the other. They wasted no time checking her out.

Arabelle darted a look at their lofty, knowing smiles. Upperclassmen for sure.

"You a ninth grader?" Jeff asked.

"Gosh, how'd you guess?"

"You look like a ninth grader," he said, jamming books, hockey stick, helmet, and skates into his locker.

She had hoped she looked older. "My name's Arabelle, but I prefer Alex." Her cheeks ached from smiling.

"That's pretty weird."

"If you want to know why — "

"Spare me," Jeff snorted, and kicked his locker door shut.

"Are you sure?"

"Yep."

Arabelle thought fast. "You must be going out for hockey," she blurted, when nothing else occurred to her. She had counted on explaining her middle name.

Jeff waggled his eyes at her. "Ya think? Yo, Bonnie, how's it goin'?" Jeff Anderson was through with her.

Bonnie Atwood — tall, blond, and tanned — joked, "Fantastic now that I'm breathing the same air as you."

Arabelle, squeezed between them, ceased to exist. She was invisible, a fate worse than death. Her five-foot-one body, small by anyone's measurement, didn't help, and neither did her wavy brown hair worn in a ponytail like a million other ninth graders. Why couldn't her eyes be green like Deirdre's instead of gray? Green eyes promised romance and adventure. In novels, the heroine always had green eyes.

"Hi, I'm Arabelle Archer but I prefer Alex." She smiled at Bonnie, determined to be visible.

Bonnie raised carefully plucked eyebrows. "Really? Well, I'm Bonnie Atwood but I prefer Bonnie."

Jeff rolled his eyes. "Save us from ninth graders."

"And girls with boys' names," Bonnie said with a tinkly laugh that sounded fake, and off they went, leaving Arabelle to her very neat and mostly empty locker, and her failed attempts to stand out. She had faced her first challenge and come up short. Trying harder was the obvious solution.

At noon, after a morning of unreasonable expectations from her teachers, starting with English, then Algebra and

Biology, Arabelle headed straight to the cafeteria. Erna Sue Comstock, the sole survivor of her inner circle, waited by the door. Three of Arabelle's closest friends had gone to Catholic school for ninth grade. She and Erna Sue had been friends since seventh grade, when they sat next to each other in Social Studies. At the time Erna Sue had just moved to town from Milwaukee and needed a friend.

Unlike the middle school cafeteria in Grafton Green, the one at James Madison was half the size of a football field. Jocks and cheerleaders claimed the best seats. Everyone else settled for second best at the long tables. The lunch line, two deep, snaked out the door, then doubled back on itself. Loud voices and shrieks of laughter filled the air.

Arabelle and Erna Sue sat together at a table populated by ninth graders.

"What're you volunteering for, Alex?"

Arabelle gazed at Erna Sue, a taco halfway to her mouth. "What d'you mean?"

"For your college application. You don't get into a good college unless you volunteer for community service."

"I don't know. I haven't thought about it."

"My first choice is working at the Grafton Green library, my second is monitoring the recycle bins at the IGA."

"What's the rush, Erna Sue? College isn't for ages."

"Alex, James Madison is a high-performing school. Four years is hardly enough time to do everything you need to get into a good college."

Arabelle almost said, "Can't you ever let things happen? Why must you always plan?" But she didn't, because Erna Sue never let things just happen.

"I've been thinking about extracurriculars. I might go out for Debating Club." Erna Sue stared at the hockey team shooting straw wrappers at the cheerleaders three tables over. "I need to sharpen my mental faculties so I don't end up like them."

"Not much danger of that," Arabelle said. Erna Sue was the smartest person she knew, not counting her own father, who was a professor at the state university.

"What are you going out for?" Erna Sue asked.

"Drama Club." Arabelle dropped her voice so no one would overhear. "I'm dying to be in the school play. What do you think my chances are?" Maybe Erna Sue would say, "Go for it, Alex!"

Erna Sue tucked her straight brown hair behind her ears. "Well, what plays have you been in?"

Arabelle slumped a little. "I was almost in *Annie*."

"Wasn't that sixth grade? I was still living in Milwaukee."

"Right, I forgot. Remember when I was in *The Sound of Music*?"

"You were Liesl —"

"No, I wasn't." How could Erna Sue forget? Arabelle toyed with her fork. "I was a nun."

"Of course, now I remember. You were — uh — good."

She had been much better than good. "Just good or better than good?"

"Uh — better."

Arabelle had hoped for more. Still, Erna Sue wasn't overly generous with compliments. When she gave one, she usually meant it.

"Isn't Drama Club mostly upperclassmen, Alex?"

"Is it? You mean I can't join?"

"Don't be silly. Joining is your constitutional right."

"I'm willing to take the smallest role. One that nobody wants." She'd start small and work her way to the top. Like Deirdre, stardom was her destiny.

"I wouldn't get my hopes up." Erna Sue pushed her glasses up on her nose. They had a way of sliding down.

"Why not?"

"You're a ninth grader, remember? Rock bottom in the pecking order."

"But what about my right as a citizen?"

"You have the right to join Drama Club, Alex. That does not guarantee you a part in the play."

By the end of lunch, Arabelle had decided to sign up. The first meeting was scheduled for that afternoon, after the final bell.

Arabelle hesitated in the doorway of the activities room as students slipped past her and found seats. Bonnie Atwood stood up front.

"Well, hey, look who's here," she chirped. "Come on in. It's Felix, isn't it? This is exciting. You're our first ninth grader. Isn't this exciting, everyone? We're dying to know why you're here."

"It — it's Alex." Arabelle swallowed hard. She had no speech prepared. Why hadn't she written one in study hall? "I'd like a part in the school play," she said, pasting on a glittering smile.

"Wouldn't we all." Bonnie traded grins with half the room.

"But I want one a lot. I plan on an acting career." Arabelle's face burned. Her words were all wrong. Deirdre Glendenning would've known just what to say.

"Freshmen don't get parts, Alex. Who remembers the last time a ninth grader was in the school play?"

No hand was raised.

"You see?" Bonnie smiled at her.

"I'm willing to take a small part," Arabelle stammered. "One or two lines are okay." How could she fulfill her destiny and be a star if she didn't have one or two lines?

Bonnie's smile didn't waver. "But we don't know what the play is. Mr. Zee hasn't decided —"

"Mr. Zee?" Arabelle racked her brain.

"The drama coach, Alex. And just so you know, I'm the president of Drama Club. At James Madison, seniors and juniors get dibs on all the parts. Freshmen wait."

"I didn't know —"

"Well, now you do." Titters ran like brush fire around the room. "But feel free to join Drama Club, Alex."

Arabelle had had enough. She had flunked her first audition. "Thanks, anyway." Summoning her brightest smile, Deirdre Alexis Glendenning turned on her heel and fled the room.

The hall outside was empty. She fought back tears. I'll show them, she vowed. One day I'll be famous and then they'll be sorry.

She resolved to try out for the play, no matter what.

The New Boy

By the end of the week, Arabelle's locker encounters with Bonnie and Jeff had settled into a familiar pattern:

"Well, hi, Felix." Bonnie smiled like a cat. She'd have cleaned her whiskers if she had any.

"Alex, Bonnie — short for Anabelle," Jeff said in mock horror. "How could you forget?"

Arabelle humored them with a smile. "Very funny, and it's Arabelle," but they weren't listening.

"Have you met the new dude, Bonnie? What's his name?"

"Not yet. Boris something — he's from Russia."

Here was the perfect opening. "Actually, he's from Ukraine," Arabelle confided. "His last name is Petrenko. He's here on a Rotary scholarship." Wonder of wonders she now had two pairs of eyes trained on her. "He's taking a postgraduate year of high school."

"How do you know that?" Bonnie asked, her eyes narrowed in suspicion.

"My English teacher introduced him in class. He sits next to me."

Jeff stared at her. "What's he doing in freshman English?"

"He needs practice reading and speaking. That's why he's here. Upper-level English is too advanced."

"Poor Boris," Bonnie murmured, "taking a class with ninth graders. I'd die." After a moment, she brightened. "Let's ask him to eat with us, Jeff. We'll help him with his English. I'll offer to help him with homework. Do you think he plays hockey?"

"Positive. Russians are star players."

"Ukrainians. He's from Ukraine," Arabelle prompted, but her brief moment in the sun was over.

Arabelle figured out at once why Bonnie and Jeff were so eager with offers of friendship. The reason was Boris Petrenko himself, a vivid presence in James Madison High after three measly days and the center of attention wherever he went, a long scarf flung around his neck and a shock of coal-black hair falling over his brow. Black eyes, too. Wicked eyes that laughed one minute and teased the next. Jeff swore that Boris was built like the perfect hockey player. Bonnie agreed. Arabelle didn't care about hockey. To her, Boris was a desert warrior straight out of a novel.

For three lunch periods in a row, Arabelle and Erna Sue

watched Bonnie drag Boris to her table and fuss over him. On the third day, the hockey players moved closer to Bonnie's table, to keep an eye on Boris and not be at a disadvantage.

"Yo, Boris!" Jeff called. "Whassup?"

By keeping her ears open and mouth shut, Arabelle had learned that Jeff Anderson was captain of the hockey team and a junior. Bonnie was a senior.

"What is yo?" Boris asked, his slice of pizza suspended midair. "Is word I not know."

Arabelle and Erna Sue exchanged a look. This should be good, they telegraphed each other.

"It's like hey," Jeff said, "or listen up."

"And other word? What means?"

"Whassup?" Jeff and his teammates traded grins. "It means 'what's goin' on?'"

Boris shook his head and burst out laughing.

"He does that when he doesn't understand," Erna Sue murmured. "Have you noticed?"

"Smiling and laughing when you don't understand is like armor. It protects you from ridicule." Hadn't Arabelle done the same a million times? And the way things were going, wouldn't she do it a million more times?

The following Monday, Arabelle took her usual seat in English. Class hadn't started.

Boris leaned across the aisle and said, "Yo, dude!" He grinned at her. "Did I say right?"

Arabelle laughed. "You sound just like Jeff." This was

the first time Boris had spoken to her. "I'm Alex," she said. "Alexis is my middle name but I've shortened it to Alex." What a relief to get that off her chest!

"My name Boris —"

"I know. Everyone in school knows who you are." A hockey star, a desert warrior, an exotic life form unlike any other at James Madison High — none of which she mentioned.

"Do you always eat lunch with Bonnie?" Arabelle hadn't meant to ask him so abruptly or so soon but excitement got the better of her.

"Da."

"How come?"

"She ask me."

"What if I asked you? What would you say?" She already knew, but it never hurt to try.

"Da."

"You mean it?" She gaped at him. "What about today? I eat with Erna Sue Comstock. She's the smartest girl in ninth grade."

"Da. Okay."

Arabelle, thrilled by his consent, would have prolonged the moment, only her teacher rapped for silence. On her way out of class, Arabelle called over her shoulder, "See you at noon, Boris." She wondered if he'd wimp out. Bonnie acted like she owned him and so far he hadn't seemed to mind.

During her free period Arabelle presented herself to her

college counselor. It was their first meeting.

"Now then, Arabelle, we need to talk about volunteer activities. Colleges place great importance on volunteering." Mrs. Peeples opened a folder on her desk, extracted a piece of paper, and slid it toward Arabelle.

"More so than grades and test scores? My father's a college professor and he says grades and scores are totally up there."

Mrs. Peeples fixed her with a steely eye. "Volunteer activities, Arabelle. I know what I'm talking about. I've been doing this job for many years."

Arabelle ran her eye down the items on the list and decided not to go to college.

1. Rake and mow lawns for the elderly
2. Work at a used clothing bank
3. Clean dog cages and cat boxes at an animal shelter
4. Monitor recycle bins at the supermarket
5. Pick up litter in public parks
6. Coach a senior citizens' volleyball team

Only someone like Mrs. Peeples, with her head of tight, gray curls on a Poppin' Fresh Doughboy body, could produce such a list.

"Well?" Mrs. Peeples was waiting.

"Can I think about it and let you know?" Arabelle looked over the list again. "What about volunteering at the Grafton Green library?"

"It's taken."

Erna Sue had wasted no time. Arabelle read through the list again. "None of these activities are very exciting."

Mrs. Peeples pressed her lips together. "Volunteering is not about excitement, Arabelle. This is an approved list. I'm confident that you and one of these activities will be a perfect fit."

Arabelle thought otherwise. She'd just have to come up with the perfect solution herself.

At noon Arabelle and Erna Sue hunched over their trays, watching Bonnie's table. Every seat, except one, was taken.

"Where's Boris?" Erna Sue asked, eyeing the empty seat next to Bonnie.

"At the end of the line." Arabelle had spotted him the moment he walked through the door. "I asked him to eat with us, Erna Sue. He's nice. We've gotten to know each other in English class."

Boris moved slowly past the salads and the steam table, laughing and joking with the lunch ladies, then stood a moment scanning the cafeteria.

Bonnie waved frantically. "Over here, Boris. I've saved a seat."

Boris shook his head. "Is okay, is okay. I no sit."

Bonnie reached him in three strides. "What do you mean?" She grabbed his arm, nearly capsizing his tray. "You can't eat standing up. It's not allowed."

"I sit there," he said. Rescuing his arm, he made straight for Arabelle.

"Wait," Bonnie yelled. "I'll join you." But she didn't when she saw where he was headed.

Boris started to put his tray down, then straightened.

The now familiar grin took over. "Please, I sit?"

Erna Sue raised her eyebrows. "Are you asking us or telling us?"

Arabelle kicked her under the table. "Have a seat, Boris, but beware! Eating with ninth graders is considered the pits."

Boris looked from one to the other, his brow knit. "Is okay?"

"Definitely okay," Arabelle said, with her most welcoming smile.

Boris set his tray down and pulled up a chair. "What means?"

"What means what?" Arabelle asked.

Erna Sue unwrapped her hoagie. "He doesn't understand 'pits,' Alex."

"Oh! Well, pits means . . . it's like the worst. Not that eating with *us* is ever the worst. But some people might think it was."

"Like Bonnie," Erna Sue said with a knowing smile.

Arabelle could tell by his laugh that Boris didn't get it.

"Yo, dudes!" Jeff Anderson hopped up on a chair and waved his arms for attention. The noise level dropped a notch. "Hockey tryouts at three. We got a star player with us this year. Let's turn out in force." Jeff's eyes settled on Boris. Boris stared at his tray.

"Where's your helmet?" Erna Sue asked him, after Jeff sat down. Hockey wannabes had worn their helmets to lunch.

"In locker."

"'In *my* locker,' not 'in locker,'" Erna Sue said.

"You hockey player?" Boris regarded Erna Sue with lively interest.

Erna Sue squinted at Arabelle. "What is he talking about?"

"You're confusing him by correcting his English."

"But that's the point of living in another country, Alex. You learn to speak the language correctly. How can you speak correctly if your grammar goes unchallenged?"

"He's doing fine," Arabelle said. "Were you a star player back home, Boris?"

"I no play hockey." Boris shrugged. "Let country down."

Arabelle shook her head at Erna Sue before she could change "I no play hockey" to "I don't play hockey" or "I'm not a hockey player."

"Does Jeff know? Have you told him?"

Boris nodded. "He no believe me."

"He doesn't believe you," Erna Sue said. "Doesn't. Does not."

"Da! He no believe me."

Arabelle mulled this over. "Why did you bring a hockey helmet all the way from Ukraine if you don't play hockey?"

"I no bring helmet. Is from Jeff. Is from school gym."

Arabelle locked eyes with Erna Sue. Though he didn't realize it, Boris was in a bit of a pickle. "So what are you going to do?" she asked.

Boris thought hard, then dug out his Russian/English pocket dictionary and flipped through the pages, searching for the word. At that moment Jeff and his hockey mates clumped by on their way out of the cafeteria.

"Yo, Boris!" Jeff clapped his new star player on the back. "We're counting on you to show us how the game's played in Russia."

Without any sign or warning, Boris staggered to his feet clutching his head with both hands, and like a gored ox crashed to the floor. Somehow he managed this very neatly, without upsetting his tray or anyone else's. And more amazing still, he managed to fall without hitting his chair or the edge of the table.

Pandemonium erupted as students leapt to their feet and rallied round. A fallen comrade lay as still as death.

"Omigosh! Omigosh!" Arabelle stooped over Boris, searching frantically for a pulse.

Erna Sue, kneeling on top of the table, issued instruction. "Check the pulse in his neck, Alex."

"Which side?"

"Left side," someone shouted.

"No, right side!"

"Either side!" Erna Sue yelled. "The pulse is on both sides, people."

"Where are the lunch monitors?"

"Out in the hall. There's a fight."

"Someone call 9-1-1!"

Boris' eyes opened slowly. Arabelle helped him sit up. "Is okay, is okay." He smiled sheepishly at the worried faces around him. "Is from hockey," he said, rubbing his head.

"What's he mean?"

"Dunno."

Arabelle handed Boris his dictionary. "See if you can find the word for what's wrong with you."

While he searched, everybody offered suggestions. "He may be diabetic. Do you need insulin, Boris?" Boris shook his head.

"Maybe he's a hemophiliac."

"What's that?"

"A disease of the blood. Russians get it."

"Hemophilia is not a disease," Erna Sue said. "It's a hereditary defect found in males. Hemophiliacs bleed to death. Obviously Boris is not a hemophiliac."

"Hah!" Jubilant, Boris jabbed at a word on the page.

"Concussion?" Arabelle lobbed question marks at Boris to make sure that's what he meant. "You're concussed?"

"Da."

"But how can you be? All you were doing was eating lunch."

"Play hockey whole life. Many concuss. In out hospital, in out, in out. No more play hockey. Concuss come much."

Jeff's mouth hung open. "You mean you pass out anywhere, anytime?"

"Da." Arabelle and Boris made brief eye contact. She detected the flicker of a smile before he looked away.

"Wow, that's tough." Jeff spoke for everyone.

Bonnie said, "That's so awful, Boris. How can you

bear it?"

"Is hard. Am sad no more play hockey."

"Of course you are," Bonnie said, helping Boris to his feet, "but you don't want to pass out and die. Hockey is not worth dying for."

"Nyet," Boris said, shaking his head, and with Bonnie's arm around his waist and trailed by Jeff and his teammates, a stricken warrior was helped from the cafeteria.

Arabelle, silent and admiring, reflected on his performance. He was more of an actor than she was. They shared a special bond. She wouldn't force a confession or let on what she knew. In his own good time, he would tell her. It was better that way.

A Terrible Request

Arabelle was sure that by weaseling out of hockey, Boris would no longer be well regarded. But his reputation soared after the incident in the cafeteria. Between them, Bonnie and Jeff elevated Boris to Olympian heights, until his fame as a hockey player was fixed forever and his fainting spells the sad, sad result of multiple concussions sustained in the sport closest to his heart.

One day before English, Arabelle brought matters to a head. She was tired of waiting for a confession that never came. "You were acting, weren't you, when you passed out in the cafeteria?"

"Da."

"But why? All you had to do was tell Jeff the truth. You don't play hockey and you don't plan to learn. Period."

Boris shrugged. "I try. Jeff no believe me. Truth is boring."

"And lies are okay if they're interesting?" She could hardly believe her ears.

"Da."

She debated asking him more, afraid of what he might say. Still . . .

"Do you lie a lot?" she asked.

"Da — yes." He teased her with his eyes.

She was sorry she'd asked, though maybe he was lying about lying.

"You shouldn't lie, Boris. You'll get into trouble."

Boris shrugged. "Everyone lie. Lie sometime truth. Truth sometime lie. Hard to tell."

Whatever that meant! Wasn't a lie false and truth true? But she didn't argue the point. The language barrier between them was too great.

Late one morning Erna Sue hailed Arabelle between classes. "Mrs. Peeples wants to see you."

"What for?" Her college counselor was the last person on earth she wanted to see.

Erna Sue didn't slow down. "About volunteering."

Arabelle groaned. The truth of the matter was this: she hadn't come up with the perfect solution and nothing on Mrs. Peeples' list tempted her to pledge four years of her life to the greater good of mankind. And now, without warning, when no meeting had been scheduled, she had to forego her one free period and face her counselor, who would expect an answer.

Mrs. Peeples was waiting for her. "The most interesting request has come across my desk, Arabelle. I thought of you immediately."

Could excitement and adventure be within reach after all? Maybe as a volunteer ambulance attendant riding in back, begging the injured to hang on, help was around the corner . . .

"What's the request?" Arabelle asked, holding her breath.

"The Heavenly Rest Nursing Home called me this morning. The director, Happy Holliday, is looking for a cheerful, outgoing teen to volunteer a few hours a week. I told her about you, and she thinks you'd be perfect."

Arabelle sagged, her hopes dashed. "I don't think so —"

"Why ever not? If I were in a nursing home, I'd rejoice at the presence of a lively, pretty girl like you."

"I don't have experience with old people. I wouldn't know how to act." Deirdre, of course, would have no trouble. She'd have them eating out of her hand.

"Nonsense. They're no different from your grandparents."

"I don't have grandparents, Mrs. Peeples. Mine are dead."

"Oh, dear, I'm so sorry. Perhaps you could think of Heavenly Rest residents as long, lost grandparents. What do you say to that?"

"I don't think so —"

"Not even on a trial basis? I told Happy Holliday I was sure you'd agree and she was going to tell her board of directors this morning at their meeting. What a huge disappointment for us all." Mrs. Peeples folded her hands and settled back in her chair.

Arabelle, at a rare loss for words, finally managed, "I'm sorry, but — but I can't."

"Then you'll have to inform Happy Holliday yourself." Mrs. Peeples yanked open a drawer. "Here's her number."

Arabelle was no match for a counselor who played hardball. Mrs. Peeples had years of experience with students like her. "Okay, I'll try it for a week." Since she had no choice, she'd pretend she was on tour with a play and the old peoples' home would be her last appearance.

Mrs. Peeples beamed. "I just know this will work out. You've got Heavenly Rest written all over you."

Arabelle banged the door on her way out.

At noon she vented to Erna Sue and Boris. Twice a week, over lunch, they helped Boris with his English. The other days Boris ate at Bonnie's table.

"Do you know what Mrs. Peeples said?" Arabelle said. "That I have Heavenly Rest written all over me. What's that supposed to mean?"

Erna Sue sniffed. "Change counselors, Alex. You have the right."

"This is high school, Erna Sue. We don't have rights."

"Please, what is 'heavenly rest'?" Boris asked.

"It's a nursing home," Arabelle said. "Old people go

there to die. No one's under a hundred, and you have to shout at them, otherwise they don't hear you. And it smells bad. I won't say in what way. Use your imagination."

Her grandpa had ended life in a nursing home. That, of course, was the one thing she remembered, together with the smell of disinfectant, and very old people slumped in their wheelchairs asleep, and wherever she looked, stained linoleum floors the color of oatmeal. She was five at the time, holding tight to her mother's hand and wishing herself a million miles away.

"Maybe not so bad," Boris said, when he finally understood what a nursing home was.

"Boris is right, Alex. You're jumping to conclusions. Wait and see. It might be better than you think."

"Have you ever been in a nursing home?" They shook their heads. "Well, I have," she said with a tight, superior smile.

"When you start?" Boris asked.

Erna Sue frowned. "When DO you start. We've been over this a million times, Boris."

"Okay, okay." He smiled at Erna Sue and got a quick smile in return.

Arabelle made a face. "Next week, I guess. Unless I come down with a fatal disease between now and then."

On her way to class, Arabelle pushed through a crowd of juniors and seniors bunched in front of the extracurricular board. "What's going on?"

"Tryouts for the school play."

"What's the play?" She was too far back to read the

32

notice pinned on the board.

Bonnie Atwood looked over her shoulder. "*You Can't Take It With You,* Felix. Remember what I said? The lead roles go to seniors and juniors. Sophomores get what's left over. Freshmen sweep the stage and paint scenery." Everyone laughed.

Arabelle suffered in silence. If Bonnie thought she'd settle for a broom or a paintbrush, she was in for a surprise.

At the end of the day Arabelle borrowed *You Can't Take It With You* from the school library. There were two copies. Boris Petrenko had the other one under his arm.

That night at dinner she blew off steam about Mrs. Peeples ruining her life. "I hate nursing homes. I'd rather swallow seeds and get appendicitis than work at Heavenly Rest."

"Seeds don't cause appendicitis," her father said, when she came up for air. A professor of ornithology at the state university, Lyman Archer was constantly correcting false information. "Why did you agree to volunteer if you feel so strongly?"

"Mrs. Peeples laid a guilt trip on me. It's so not fair."

Her mother weighed in. "You loved your visits to Grandpa, Arabelle."

"Not when he was in that nursing home, I didn't."

"But you did, sweetie, you've just forgotten."

"No, I haven't! You've forgotten! That first visit was awful. I'll never forget it. That's why I refused to go back."

Mrs. Archer shook her head. One of them was crazy.

"You visited Grandpa in his nursing home several times, Arabelle. Didn't she, Lyman?" Her father was often called on to cast deciding votes.

"I don't recall the number, Marian."

"Grandpa adored you, sweetie. Don't you remember?"

"No." She didn't want to talk about her grandpa. She didn't want to remember him on the floor with a crowd around him, or what had happened afterward.

Her mom laughed. She always laughed when she talked about Grandpa. "He often wondered how your father and I ever produced such a high-spirited, actressy daughter when we were so — so —"

"Square," her father said, finishing her sentence. He did that a lot. Her mother didn't seem to mind. Arabelle couldn't imagine why.

"You loved riding in Grandpa's wheelchair. Surely you remember that."

"Well, I don't, Mom, okay?" And she didn't wish to be reminded.

"It's no longer important," her father said, "and it is certainly not worth arguing about."

Although Arabelle knew where the truth of the matter lay and who was right about visits to Grandpa in his wretched nursing home, the less said about her grandpa, the better.

Later that night, Arabelle read *You Can't Take It With You*. The play was funnier than she expected. Never had she met a crazier bunch of people. She tried to figure out which part Bonnie had her eye on. Probably young, beautiful Alice Sycamore, in love with nice, clean-cut Tony Kirby. Boris, of course, had to play Kolenkhov, the Russian ballet teacher. The part was made for him.

Essie Carmichael was the role she'd try out for. Essie was a ballet dancer, though not a very good one. In fact she was terrible, but funny. Arabelle closed her eyes and, for one magic moment, imagined leaping and twirling around stage to laughter and applause. If given half a chance, she could be the star of the show. Instead she was a lowly ninth grader, and she didn't toe dance — not even badly. Somehow she had to find a way. She'd show Bonnie and the doubters in Drama Club what she was made of. See if she wouldn't.

Heavenly Rest

The next day at lunch Bonnie Atwood jumped up on her chair and waved her arms. "Seniors and juniors, listen up! Anyone trying out for the school play, please meet at my table. We need to make sure we don't audition for the same parts. No overlaps allowed. We mustn't confuse Mr. Zee." This sparked laughter. "Sophomores, you can try out for the parts we don't want. Freshmen, stay away! Your turn will come, unless you repeat ninth grade." More laughs.

"It's your right to try out for Essie, Alex. There's nothing Bonnie can do."

Arabelle had just finished describing the play to Erna Sue. "Essie's a ballet dancer. I don't toe dance."

"Try out for a different part."

"I don't want a different part. Essie and I are made for each other."

"Not if you don't toe dance." Erna Sue was like a splash of cold water.

Arabelle wavered. Maybe no one would care if she couldn't dance. "I'll audition if you do, Erna Sue." Strength lay in numbers.

"No way, Alex. I'm not into acting. Besides, Mr. Zee will need an assistant to take notes during rehearsal. I plan to offer my services." When it came to note-taking, Erna Sue Comstock was without equal.

"What should I do?" Arabelle moaned. A field mouse had more gumption. Deirdre would know just what to do.

"I told you. Try out for another part."

"I could take ballet lessons."

"There isn't time, Alex."

"What about a crash course? There must be crash courses in dance."

"I doubt it."

Arabelle gave up on Erna Sue. She'd solve the problem by herself.

Boris was eating with Bonnie at a table nearby. Arabelle, who faced in their direction, relayed the play-by-play action to Erna Sue, whose back was to them.

"Bonnie has her arm around Boris's neck. She's going to kiss him, I swear."

Erna Sue glanced over her shoulder. "Gross. Tell me when it's over."

"Not yet."

"Are they kissing?"

"Almost."

With a laugh, Boris ducked out from under Bonnie's arm and gathered up his tray.

Arabelle exhaled. "It's safe. You can look."

"Did he kiss her?"

"No. I don't think he wanted to." Arabelle cast a glance at her best friend, who until now had never cared about who kissed whom. They watched Boris leave the cafeteria by himself.

"Boris will need our help with English if he's in the play," Erna Sue said.

"His lines sound like the way he talks, but he may need help with chest hair."

"Excuse me?"

"Kolenkhov is supposed to have a very hairy chest. Those are the play directions. He takes his shirt off in the second act."

"Play directions can be ignored, Alex. I don't think you have much chest hair at Boris's age."

Arabelle couldn't imagine how Erna Sue assumed this since she didn't have an older brother to consult.

"Does Kolenkhov or anyone else have lines that refer to his chest hair?" Erna Sue asked, her eyes lowered.

"Not that I remember."

"Then chest hair and whether there's enough is not a problem."

"Tryouts at three in the auditorium," Bonnie yelled on her way out of the cafeteria. "Don't be late. We don't want Mr. Zee mad at us."

"Oh, no!" Arabelle suddenly remembered where she'd

be. "I can't make it at three."

"Heavenly Rest?"

"My first day. I'll miss tryouts."

"You better settle for prompting, Alex."

"I'll tell Happy I can't make it."

"Bad move! You can try out for the play next year."

"But what about Essie?"

"Get real, Alex. There's no way you can play Essie. You don't dance. I'll tell Mr. Zee you want to prompt."

Arabelle weighed her options. Prompting might not be so bad after all. She remembered opening night of *The Sound of Music*. Gripped by stage fright, Maria and the Captain had forgotten their lines, and Maria froze mid-song when she got her favorite things mixed up. *You Can't Take It With You* would be no different. Arabelle would feed lines to the memory challenged — entire speeches if she had to — and save the show. She would be the best prompter that James Madison High ever had.

"Make sure your hours at Heavenly Rest don't conflict with rehearsals, Alex."

Play rehearsals were always after school. Which meant volunteering on weekends, a prospect that left Arabelle far from thrilled.

Heavenly Rest Nursing Home occupied a modern brick building on the outskirts of town. It looked more like an apartment house than a nursing home to Arabelle, and from the outside at least, a pleasant place to live. Patches of rhododendron and mountain laurel bordered the sweeping lawn, nipped in spots by early frost. Nearby, brightly colored leaves floated on the surface of a reflecting pool. The only sound was the sad call of mourning doves.

Arabelle tucked her bike behind a hedge and stood a moment preparing for her entrance. "You can do this, Alex," she whispered. "Pretend you're Deirdre and this is your final performance in a play that's about to fold."

On her way to the front door, she passed a frowning old man bundled in a winter coat and sitting in a wheelchair.

"What d'you want?" he growled.

"I'm here to see Happy Holliday." She smiled brightly.

"What you smiling at?"

"I'm just being friendly."

"Waste of time, smiling. What'd you say your name was?"

"It's Arabelle."

"What?"

"ARABELLE!" Her impression of nursing homes was now doubly confirmed: havens for the old, the deaf, and the crabby.

Inside, a receptionist wearing a lei of artificial orchids peered at her over a computer screen. "Yes?"

"I have an appointment with Happy Holliday."

The receptionist smiled. "You must be the little high schooler that's going to help out."

Arabelle stiffened. She was not little, she was short. Why couldn't people tell the difference?

"You'll find Miss Holliday in the Aloha wing. Go through the double doors and follow the pineapples painted on the floor." She pressed a button and the two swinging doors slowly opened. Arabelle didn't exactly dance through.

The nurses' station was straight ahead. "I'm looking for Happy Holliday," she told the nurse on duty.

"You must be the lit —"

"Volunteer! I'm the volunteer."

"Aloha wing. Follow the —"

"Pineapples?"

The nurse regarded her crossly.

"Just making sure," Arabelle said. "I don't want to be late for my 3:00 appointment."

"You're already late. Fifteen minutes by that clock." They both glanced at the giant clock on the wall behind the nurses' desk. She was not off to a good start.

At a crossroads, where pineapples intersected with bananas and snow-capped mountains, Arabelle turned right and started down a long corridor with grip bars on either side. The linoleum was sea green — an improvement on oatmeal, but not by much. The walls, covered with murals of palm trees bending in the wind, featured smiling natives in grass skirts strumming ukeleles. The pungent smell of Lysol reminded her that she was not in Hawaii.

"Help me! Help me!" a man called from a darkened room.

Just as she feared — the torture chamber doing its grisly work. Curious, she peered through the open door.

The victim, sitting on the side of his bed, wore a full suit of clothes and a straw hat. "Help me! Help me!" he begged.

"What's wrong?"

"Help me! Help me!"

Arabelle hovered in the doorway. What should she do? "I'll call a nurse." Deirdre would've flown to his side.

"Help me! Help me!"

Arabelle darted into the corridor and hailed a nurses' aide passing by. "Excuse me, I think this man needs help."

"Mr. Wexler? He don't need help, honey. He says, 'help me, help me' all day long. First thing when he wakes up, last thing before he goes to bed. It's his way. You must be new around here."

"I didn't know," she stammered. "I'm looking for Happy Holliday. Is she around?"

"She's in Miz Cushman's room. End of the hall, last door on the right."

Arabelle was alone in the corridor and unprepared when an inmate — for that's how she thought of the residents — strolled from his room. This one wore socks and sandals and not another stitch.

Do not panic, she told herself. You've seen naked men before. Offhand she couldn't remember where. The museum, probably. There was only one thing to do: close her eyes tight and go by quickly.

She heard him say "Good afternoon" as they passed each other.

The nurses' aide from before appeared suddenly and swooped down on him. "Shame on you, Mr. Rosen.

Where are your clothes? You'll catch your death bare naked like that."

"So sorry, so sorry, I forgot."

When Arabelle dared to look, the corridor was blessedly empty. Wasting no more time, she reached Mrs. Cushman's room without further mishap. So far, her second-ever experience in a nursing home had surpassed her first in awfulness.

Happy Holliday was knee to knee with Mrs. Cushman, who sat in a wheel chair, an afghan tucked around her.

"You must be Arabelle!" Happy beamed at her as if she was the most important person on earth. "Welcome to Heavenly Rest. I was just telling Mrs. Cushman about you. We're thrilled you're here, aren't we, Mrs. Cushman?" Mrs. Cushman stared straight ahead without moving or blinking.

Happy Holliday looked about her mom's age, with frizzy red hair and eyes as blue as a lagoon. Arabelle mustered a smile. The open, friendly face was hard to resist.

"You must be wondering about my name. Mrs. Cushman wondered about that too when she joined us — how many years ago was it, Mrs. Cushman?" Mrs. Cushman stared into space.

"I like to trot it out first thing," Happy said with a laugh. "Most people are too polite to ask."

Mrs. Cushman still hadn't blinked or moved a muscle. The only sign of life was the rise and fall of her chest. Arabelle dragged her eyes away and concentrated on

Happy's sunny smile and sparkly eyes.

"Happy isn't my real name, Arabelle."

"I guessed it wasn't."

"Holliday isn't either."

"It isn't?"

"My birth name is Mona Stunker. Now I ask you, how can such a name cheer people up or fill them with hope for a brighter tomorrow? For most of our residents, Heavenly Rest Nursing Home is the last stop before heaven. We strive to make their final days on earth carefree and happy, the way a holiday is. That's why I changed my name to Happy Holliday." She paused.

Arabelle groped for words. "Is that why this is called the Aloha wing?"

Happy twinkled at Mrs. Cushman. "Didn't I tell you she'd pick up on that?" Mrs. Cushman blinked. A milestone!

"Are the bananas and the snowy mountains wings too?" Arabelle asked.

"Bless your heart. You are an observant one. The bananas lead to our Caribbean wing and the snow-capped mountains to the Shangri-la wing. I named the wings myself when I became director."

"But isn't Shangri-la an imaginary place?"

For the first time since Arabelle entered the room, Happy stopped smiling. "It exists here," she said gravely. "Make no mistake. Shangri-la is alive and well at Heavenly Rest."

Arabelle didn't see how. Her experience had been the

exact opposite of Shangri-la. "Can you tell me what my duties will be, Ms. Holliday —"

"Please call me Happy, Arabelle."

"When do you want me to start? I have play rehearsals after school and homework at night."

Maybe, just maybe, her services wouldn't be needed. If only Happy weren't so nice, Arabelle would tell her that old people made her uneasy and that Mrs. Cushman scared her a little and Mr. Rosen scared her a lot and if there were more like them, she wouldn't last a week.

Her thoughts must have raced across her face, because Happy said, "I know how you feel. Nursing homes take getting used to. Mrs. Cushman has Alzheimer's and she takes getting used to."

Arabelle's heart foundered. "How many Alzheimer's patients are there?" Maybe Mrs. Cushman was the only one.

"A few, all in various stages of the disease. Every single one is a unique, beautiful human being."

"I could do Saturday mornings, I guess." Please, please say no, Arabelle prayed.

"Perfect!"

Too late to back out. "Maybe on a trial basis, to start with? You may not want me for good."

"Our residents thrive on a daily routine, Arabelle. They won't understand if you start with them, then fail to show up. Showing up is important."

Happy planted a farewell kiss on Mrs. Cushman's brow. Arabelle followed her out to the hall. She still didn't know what her duties were.

"Gwenda Watkins, our tireless social director, needs an extra hand. She goes off duty at three, otherwise I'd introduce you. How are we today, Mr. Wexler?" Mr. Wexler was standing in his doorway.

"Help me! Help me!"

"Help is on the way," Happy called over her shoulder. She turned to Arabelle. "Social activities are important at Heavenly Rest. Having fun is important. You and Gwenda together can make Saturday mornings the high point of the week for our residents. Just think of that!"

Happy slowed her steps as an old woman in a flowing white gown staggered into the hall.

"'Hey non nonny, nonny, hey nonny,'" the old lady cried, plucking at her hair. "'I would give you some violets but they withered all when my father died.'"

"Mrs. Becker is an actress, Arabelle." Happy raised her voice several notches. "Are we Ophelia today, Camille?"

"Oh, damn! How'd you guess? I was about to launch into my mad scene."

"Where's your walker, Camille? You shouldn't be out without your walker."

"Fiddledeedee!" Mrs. Becker looked Arabelle over with the eyes of a hawk. "Who is this perfectly lovely child, Happy?"

Arabelle took a step back. Mrs. Becker was much too old to play Ophelia. Didn't she know better? "My name's Arabelle."

"How poetic!" Mrs. Becker clutched her heart. "I believe in poetic names, don't you?"

Arabelle opened her mouth. When nothing came out, she closed it.

"Arabelle is Gwenda's new helper, Camille. Saturday mornings she'll help Gwenda with sing-along and bat-the-ball and armchair aerobics."

"What about Mah-Jongg? I won't come if there's no Mah-Jongg."

"Mah-Jongg is Thursday nights, Camille. Not everyone plays it. Saturday morning activities should include everyone."

Arabelle stewed in silence. Her only thought now was escape from Heavenly Rest and its human relics. She had tried her best with them, but they had defeated her. She had bombed in her final performance. Erna Sue was right. For someone who didn't dance and hadn't a shred of acting talent, prompting was the only answer.

At the far end of the hall, residents gathered outside the dining room.

"What's for dinner?" Mrs. Becker cried. She had found her walker and was thumping down the hall at warp speed.

"Mealtime is big around here," Happy confided. "Wheelchairs and walkers start lining up half an hour before the dinner gong sounds. Perhaps you'll join us —"

"I'm sorry, I can't. My parents expect me home for dinner." She wasn't a bit sorry.

"Then we'll see you Saturday morning," Happy said. "Don't write us off too soon, Arabelle. Give us a chance to show you the hidden gold."

Arabelle didn't want to mine for gold or be cajoled like an Alzheimer's patient. She wanted to be treated like she had her whole life ahead of her, which wouldn't end for a long, long time — and when it did, it wouldn't be in a place like the Heavenly Rest Nursing Home.

Desperate to be gone, Arabelle flew by the nurses' station, through the double doors, past the startled receptionist, and out into the crisp sanity of the autumn afternoon.

"Pants on fire, Clarabelle?" the old man in the wheel-chair yelled.

She didn't answer because she'd never see him again. Nor would she see Gwenda Watkins Saturday morning for sing-along, bat-the-ball, and armchair aerobics.

She was definitely sure about that.

Mr. Zee

At lunch the next day Erna Sue and Boris convinced Arabelle to think twice before she quit a job she hadn't even started.

"When Mrs. Peeples finds out you've bailed," Erna Sue said, "she'll make a note in your folder. That note will follow you the rest of your life. It's like a bad credit rating."

"Da," Boris said, after Erna Sue explained what credit rating was.

"Once a week won't kill you, Alex."

"Easy for you to say," Arabelle muttered, poking at her broccoli.

"You want to be wimp?" Wimp was currently Boris's favorite word.

"Oh, all right. I'll try it for a week."

"Two weeks," Erna Sue said. "One week isn't enough."

Boris nodded. "Erna right."

"Is right," Erna Sue scolded. "Is! Is! I've explained the subject-predicate rule twice, Boris. I expect you to remember."

"Okay, okay." Boris sighed. "Miss home so much."

Arabelle sent Erna Sue silent death threats. "Why are you so harsh? Boris is doing great."

"I'm not harsh, Alex. I'm straightforward. I don't gloss the truth. Boris understands that, don't you, Boris?"

"Da. You teach me good. No let me be lazy." He and Erna Sue shared a smile.

"By the way, Alex, you need to try out for prompter," Erna Sue said.

"I have to audition?" Since when did prompters audition?

"Mr. Zee said. Trish Vogel tried out for prompter yesterday."

A competitor was the last thing Arabelle expected. Trish was a friend of Bonnie's. Trish was a senior. Trish was blond. Still, Mr. Zee hadn't made Trish prompter. Not yet. He wanted to hear Arabelle before he decided.

Her spirits rose, then plummeted. She'd have to be better than Trish.

Arabelle shut her eyes. Please, please, make me the best prompter that ever lived, a prompter that James Madison High will be proud of, amen.

"I try out for Kolenkhov, Alex."

"Boris was amazing," Erna Sue said. "After he read the part, he got a standing ovation. Didn't you, Boris?"

"Da — yes. Everyone clap. Erna Sue clap, too."

"Did anyone clap for Trish?" Arabelle asked. Erna Sue and Boris shook their heads, which made her feel better. "When do we find out who plays what part?"

"Mr. Zee said he'd post the cast on the activities board."

"I play Kolenkhov," Boris bragged. "Mr. Zee telled me."

"Told me," Erna Sue murmured. "Past tense of to tell."

"I wonder who's playing Essie Carmichael," Arabelle said, but neither Erna Sue nor Boris could tell her.

Between classes, Arabelle and Erna Sue checked the activities board. The list was up, though they had to wait for the lucky chosen — Bonnie among them — to finish celebrating with high fives in front of the board.

"I have the lead role," Bonnie gloated, slapping palms with her two best friends.

"You've got one of the leads," Chip Wittington said. "There's more than one." Chip was president of Student Council.

"And you and I have them, Chip darling. I didn't mean to leave you out."

"I don't consider myself a lead, Bonnie. I'm not on stage that much."

"Anyone who's in love with me is a lead player," Bonnie quipped, which drew shrieks of laughter from her groupies and a faint smile from Chip.

"I was right," Arabelle whispered to Erna Sue. "Bonnie's playing Alice Sycamore. Chip must be Tony Kirby, who's in love with Alice."

"Guess who's playing Kolenkhov?" Bonnie cried. Everyone laughed. "Boris will upstage us if we're not careful. Remember, we don't want him to get all the applause."

"What a witch!" Arabelle said under her breath. She still didn't know who Essie Carmichael was until the crowd broke up, leaving the bulletin board to her and Erna Sue.

Her eyes went straight to Kyra Einstad. At 4'9" Kyra was the smallest girl in high school. She was also a gymnast. Arabelle would have been laughed off stage if she had tried out for Essie. She read through the rest of the cast. "I don't know most of them, do you, Erna Sue?" All the actors except one were juniors and seniors. The lone sophomore, Lizbeth Keppler, played boozy Gay Wellington, a small but juicy part.

"Not yet, Alex. Six weeks from now we'll know more than we want about every single one."

After her last class of the day, Arabelle found an empty table at the library and opened *Les Misérables*. She had half an hour to kill until rehearsal.

. . . Deirdre Glendenning strode down the aisle of the Drury Lane Theatre in London. Clad in breeches and a cloak, her red hair woven in a plait, she drew every eye on stage.

"What means this?" the director cried, eyeing the tall beauty daringly dressed as a man.

"I have come to audition, sir. You are seeking an actress to play Isabella in The Fatal Marriage. *Search no further. You have found her."*

"We shall see what we shall see," the director said,

pondering her words. "Read from this script, Deirdre Glendenning. Show us your destiny. Make me a believer . . ."

Arabelle gazed out the window. Deirdre's destiny was never in doubt, not from the first page. But suppose Deirdre had been made a prompter? What then? Wouldn't she have proved a brilliant prompter, and didn't brilliant prompters turn into great actresses?

On her way to the auditorium, Arabelle stopped by her locker. A cheerleader named Kiki was leaning against it. Two other cheerleaders, whose names she didn't know, hung like wash off Jeff Anderson.

"Excuse me," she said to Kiki.

Kiki didn't move. "Put that one up, Jeff. That one is so-o-o cool."

The others agreed. "Awesome. Totally."

Jeff was pasting photos of himself in pads and helmet on the inside of his locker door.

"Excuse me."

"Which one?" Grinning at his fans, Jeff held up two glossy photos of himself. An action shot and a posed shot.

"That one," the girls said, pointing to Jeff body-checking an opponent.

"How about this one?" It showed Jeff hoisted on the shoulders of his teammates.

"Way cool."

Since Kiki wasn't about to move, Arabelle nudged her.

"Hey!"

"You're blocking my locker. I need to get into it."

"You might try 'excuse me.'"

"I did. Twice."

Arabelle spun the dial and yanked the door open. Jeff hadn't looked at her once. He rarely did anymore. To Kiki and the wraparounds, she was invisible — even after "excuse me" twice. Tossing in her book bag, she slammed the door shut. "I like the slap-shot pic best," she called over her shoulder.

If they heard, they didn't let on.

Walt Zacharias was arranging chairs on stage when Arabelle arrived. She marched down the aisle and presented herself.

"I'm Arabelle, Mr. Zee. Erna Sue says you want me to audition." She sounded far braver than she felt.

During the school year Walt Zacharias taught AP French and coached drama at James Madison High. Arabelle had learned through the grapevine that he was also a popular actor in local summer theater, celebrated for his Friar Tuck in *Robin Hood* and Cowardly Lion in *The Wiz*. Students swore that Mr. Zee could do no wrong, on stage or off. His gruff manner and dramatic outbursts were considered harmless eccentricities that livened up the classroom and the hallways.

Mr. Zee was in his shirtsleeves rolled above the elbows. His mop of gray hair flew in a million directions from running his fingers through it. "Later, Arabelle. Actors are about to read their lines." He jumped off the stage and thrust a playbook at her. "Sit down and pay attention.

Where's Erna Sue?"

"Right here." Erna Sue, equipped with a notepad and flashlight, signaled from several rows back. The auditorium was in semi-darkness.

One by one members of the cast found seats on the brightly lit stage and opened their playbooks to the first act. Bonnie made Kyra Einstad move so she could sit between Chip and Boris.

"Begin!" Mr. Zee commanded. He settled down next to Erna Sue.

Arabelle sat in the front row, the script on her lap, and followed along with her finger.

The read-through proceeded at a halting pace, hampered by "ums" and "uhs." Eventually, agonizingly, they reached the last two lines of the play, spoken by Bonnie and Chip. Death from sunburn was faster. Silence fell.

Mr. Zee shifted in his seat. "That was *merde*. My dog reads better." *Merde* was Mr. Zee's favorite French word, uttered loudly and often.

Bonnie jumped to her feet. "Mr. Zee, I have a few ideas about how we can improve."

"No doubt. But I'm the director, Bonnie. I call the shots."

Bonnie sat down.

Mr. Zee strode down the aisle and planted himself in front of the stage, his hands on his hips. "Tomorrow we block, the day after tomorrow we block, the day after the day after tomorrow we walk through our parts —"

Boris raised his hand. "Please, what is block?"

"It's charting movements on stage." Mr. Zee looked in turn at each member of the cast. "I expect all of you to know your lines from the first act by next Monday. No excuses."

Everyone, except Chip, groaned. In Arabelle's experience, leaders like Chip Wittington didn't groan. Not out loud.

Mr. Zee looked over his shoulder. "Erna Sue, stand up." Erna Sue scrambled to her feet. "Erna Sue Comstock will be by my side at every rehearsal, recording my comments about your performance and how to improve it."

Bonnie waved her hand. "What's Alex doing here, Mr. Zee? Is she in the play? I don't remember seeing her name in the cast."

Frowning slightly, Mr. Zee rubbed his jaw. "Who's Alex?"

"It's me," Arabelle said in a tiny voice. She slid lower in her seat.

"Arabelle is trying out for prompter," Mr. Zee said.

"But what about Trish?" Bonnie cried. "I thought Trish was prompter."

"I haven't decided. I want Arabelle to read before I decide."

"We won't hear a word she says, Mr. Zee. Trish Vogel would be much better. I mean, you can hear Trish. What if I forget my lines?"

"You can stand on stage 'til you remember them. Any more questions?"

Kyra Einstad raised her hand. "I don't have ballet

slippers."

Arabelle chewed on her lip. Gymnasts are brave and take risks. But this was a high-wire act without a net.

Mr. Zee frowned. "You told me you toe dance, Kyra."

"I do, but not lately. Not for several years."

"Get yourself shoes. Drama Club will pay you back. Anyone else have a problem?" No one else had. "Go on, get outta here, all of you. Arabelle, stay behind."

Her heart stopped, then bucked like a mule.

Chip Wittington touched her arm in passing. "His bark's worse than his bite, Alex."

She followed Mr. Zee up on stage, her mule in full gallop. "The prompter sits in the wings," he told her, "in sight of the actors, but hidden from the audience."

Somehow she managed a smile.

"Let me hear your voice," he said, bounding out on stage. "Bottom of page twenty-six. I'll read Grandpa's heart-to-heart with God. When I dry up in the middle, I want you to prompt me."

She nodded and cleared her throat. Like Deirdre, she would make a believer of him.

Mr. Zee took center stage. "'Well, Sir,'" he read, "'we've been getting along pretty good for quite a while now, and we're certainly much obliged. Remember . . .'"

Arabelle glanced up from the page. Mr. Zee was waiting.

In a voice that rang with emotion, Arabelle held forth to an imaginary balcony. She was Deirdre and this was Drury Lane. "'All we ask is to just go along and be happy in our own sort of way —'"

"Arabelle, just the first three or four words."

"Is that enough?"

"More than enough."

One line later, Mr. Zee dried up again.

"'Of course we want to keep our health,'" she prompted, impaling herself on every word.

Mr. Zee held up a hand, his eyes closed. "Thank you, Arabelle, that'll do."

She joined him on stage. "Was I okay?" She knew she wasn't even close. Maybe he'd give her a second chance. "I can do better."

"Why didn't you try out for the play?" Mr. Zee asked, puzzling over her.

"I'm in ninth grade. I have to wait."

"Since when?"

"Don't I? Bonnie said seniors and juniors get dibs on all the parts. Freshmen paint."

"I try to accommodate upperclassmen, Arabelle, but no one has dibs. I'm sorry you didn't try out."

"I can be prompter — unless you want Trish." Her voice trailed off.

"I'll let you know tomorrow."

She followed him out of the auditorium but stayed well back so he wouldn't talk to her and see the tears in her eyes.

Her parents had started dinner by the time she got home. "I'm not hungry," she said, slumping in the doorway.

"I'll eat later. I have a ton of homework."

"But we want to hear about the play," her mother said.

"The play doesn't matter anymore. I won't be part of it."

"I thought you were prompter, sweetie."

"Trish Vogel is going to be prompter."

"Did Mr. Zee tell you that?" her father asked.

"He didn't have to. I bombed so bad when I read. He probably won't let me sweep the stage."

Her parents exchanged a look. "Why don't you come and sit down," her father said.

She dragged herself to the table and sat, her eyes filled with tears. "Why isn't there one thing I do well? It's so not fair! I hate ninth grade!"

"You do many things well," her father said quietly.

"Like what? Name one thing."

"You're good at science — better than a lot of my students — and you're a first-rate birder."

"No one cares about birds, Daddy, and I'm getting a B in Biology."

"You're the best daughter in the world, sweetie. And you have a wonderful sense of humor, doesn't she, Lyman?"

"That's an attribute, Mom. You don't do attributes."

She gazed at her parents through her tears, touched and shamed by their distress and their failed attempts to make her feel better. It was no use. They didn't understand and they never would.

A Second Chance

The next morning Arabelle shoved Deirdre into her sweater drawer and returned the dust jacket to her mother's edition of *Les Misérables*. Then she got on the bus. She was through with Deirdre. From now on she would read books about losers who end up dying in the gutter.

Jeff Anderson was at his locker when she showed up at school.

"Hi, Jeff," she said. She didn't expect an answer because he rarely gave one.

He rolled his eyes at her. "How's it goin', uh — uh —"

"Alex."

"Right. Short for — uh —"

"Alexander Graham Bell!"

Jeff laughed and looked right at her. "What d'ya know, it cracks jokes."

"I have many talents, Jeff."

"Yeah? Like what?"

She thought fast. "I can recite the Gettysburg address, word for word —"

"Awesome," Jeff said, clearly unawed.

"— while standing on my head."

He rewarded her with another laugh. After weeks of non-personhood, she was suddenly on his radar screen — the Kiki of the moment. For how long remained to be seen.

Mr. Zee hailed her between classes. "Arabelle, we need to talk." They stood in the middle of the hall while students streamed by them. "You still want to prompt?"

"Well, sure, but —"

"Trish has a schedule conflict for the next two weeks. I can't go without a prompter that long."

Arabelle hid her disappointment. She was second choice. "If you think I'm good enough."

"You'll be fine. Keep your voice steady and don't dramatize."

"I got carried away. Am I temporary prompter or permanent?"

"Permanent. Trish understands."

Arabelle fretted through Algebra, dreading what Bonnie would say when she found out. Of course there was nothing Bonnie could do. Mr. Zee had made up his mind and that was that. She hoped.

Mr. Zee made the announcement at rehearsal. "I've asked Arabelle to be our prompter. If you forget your line, she'll feed you the first three or four words. She will not provide the speech that you've failed to memorize. Am I clear?" Heads nodded. "Good. I'd like you to do one other job, Arabelle."

Her heart taxied down the runway. Mr. Zee needed her!

"There are a number of off-stage explosions in this play. Think you can handle fireworks along with prompting?"

"Oh gosh, yes." This was not the time to hesitate or let on that her only experience with explosives was sparklers on the 4th of July.

"The explosions are recorded, Arabelle. Your job is to cue up the sound effects."

"I can do that," she said with a quick grin. Though she wasn't in the cast, she felt suddenly important to the success of the play. Putting her in charge of explosives meant only one thing: Mr. Zee believed in her, Mr. Zee trusted her. She would not let him down.

She sat in the audience watching him work with his actors, showing them where to stand and move on stage. Since they were still reading from their scripts, her prompting services weren't needed. Next Monday they would need a prompter.

At the end of an hour Mr. Zee said, "Let's take a break." Arabelle was in the lobby when Bonnie stopped her. "Well, congratulations, Alex. I'll bet you're thrilled."

Arabelle scanned every syllable, every gesture for sincerity.

"I'm really glad for you," Bonnie gushed. "Trish is, too."

"She is?"

"Of course. Trish felt terrible about bailing out on Mr. Zee. You saved her life."

"I did?" As hard as she tried, Arabelle couldn't detect one false note, but that didn't mean there weren't any.

"You sure did." Bonnie laid her hand on Arabelle's arm. "Just between us — I wouldn't want this to get out, Alex — but you should know that I'm a little deaf in my left ear."

"You are?" Despite Bonnie's earnest gaze, Arabelle didn't believe a word.

"I hope you'll remember that when I need a prompt. I'm counting on you, Alex. We all are." Bonnie squeezed her arm as if they were best buds and disappeared into the auditorium.

On the late bus home, Arabelle had plenty of time to examine Bonnie's motives. Bonnie wanted her to fail — that much was clear. Bonnie would pretend not to hear the prompt unless Arabelle shouted at her. After two weeks of shouting, Mr. Zee would replace Arabelle with Trish and by some miracle Bonnie would recover her hearing.

But suppose Bonnie was telling the truth. Lots of kids her age blasted music into their ears 24/7. Weren't her own parents constantly at her about turning down the volume? Maybe Bonnie was hard of hearing. But why in her left ear? Why not in both ears?

Because, dummy, on stage an actor's left ear is closest

to the prompter. Arabelle smiled. Bonnie's deception was so obvious. Still, to be on the safe side, she'd give Bonnie the benefit of the doubt. She'd meet friendliness with friendliness. She'd go the extra mile to help Bonnie remember her lines, if she could figure out a way between now and next Monday. She closed her eyes. She always thought better with her eyes closed.

"You getting off or staying the night?" the bus driver yelled over his shoulder.

Arabelle struggled from her seat. She was his last passenger. "Sorry, I didn't mean to hold you up." The doors slammed shut behind her. One of these days he'd close them before she jumped clear.

She found her parents in the kitchen. "Guess what?" she said, hanging in the doorway.

"You're in the play?" Mrs. Archer said, her face alight.

"I'm the prompter. Mr. Zee asked me this morning."

Mrs. Archer turned off the oven and held out her arms. "I'm not surprised, sweetie. I had a hunch. Isn't this terrific news, Lyman?"

"Capital." Brief and to the point, as usual. Overstatement was not in her father's nature, but Arabelle knew he was pleased and, in his own way, proud of her.

Mr. Archer took a sip of his wine. "What happened to the other girl?"

"Trish. She has a conflict. Mr. Zee says I'll be great." Her mother's arms around her still felt good. Being fussed over always felt good. "I plan to be the best prompter Mr.

Zee has ever had. Next year I'll try out for the play. What's for dinner?"

Her mother removed a succulent roast, potatoes and onions tucked around it, from the oven. An apple cobbler, still warm, sat on the counter. On a hunch, her mother had prepared a feast in her honor.

Over dinner Arabelle tried to describe *You Can't Take It With You* to her parents.

"It's about the Sycamore family. The Sycamores are completely weird. They hang out together in a big house in New York City and do just what they want."

Her mother brightened. "That sounds like fun. Doesn't that sound like fun, Lyman?"

"Possibly."

"None of the Sycamores work or hold jobs —"

"How do they manage without an income?" Mr. Archer asked, buttering a roll.

"I don't know, Daddy, they just do. Alice works. She's a secretary —"

"Secretaries don't earn much," Mr. Archer said. "How many people is she supporting?"

How typical of her father. "Seven, I think."

"Impossible on a secretary's salary."

"Lyman, let her finish. Go on, sweetie."

"Essie's my favorite. She's a ballet dancer."

Her father frowned. "That's two incomes. Still not enough."

"Essie's not paid, Daddy. She's not a good enough dancer."

"Is there anyone who's reliable?" Mr. Archer asked, after Arabelle finished describing the cast.

"Alice is. So is Tony. They're in love."

"Not exactly proof of reliability," her father remarked.

Arabelle described the plot as best she could. She thought better than to mention the G-men or the explosions at the end of the second act and risk a further grilling.

Judging by the puzzled looks from her parents, she knew she wasn't making much sense. Well, that wasn't her fault. Blame it on the playwrights.

"Perhaps we've missed something," Mr. Archer mused.

"It's hard to explain, Daddy. You have to see it."

"Don't tell us the ending, Arabelle," her mother said. "We want to be surprised."

Mr. Archer folded his napkin and pushed back from the table. "Frankly, we're already surprised that this play was ever published, let alone put on stage."

"Well, it has been, Daddy. A million times."

Before she went to bed, Arabelle retrieved Deirdre from her dresser drawer. She would give Deirdre a second chance. It was the least she could do, considering Mr. Zee had done the same for her.

A Promise Kept

Saturday morning and Heavenly Rest came too soon. Arabelle was tempted to call in sick. Instead, she pulled on jeans and her Sierra Club hoodie, tuned out her mother's pep talk while she ate breakfast, and with hopes high, checked to see if her bike had been stolen overnight. No such luck. Thirty minutes later, she pedaled up the drive to Heavenly Rest. Not a wheelchair in sight. So far, so good.

There was no one at the reception desk when she let herself in. A cleaning woman on her way out held the double doors to the resident area open for her. The nurses' station was also vacant. With a shrinking heart Arabelle kept walking, on the lookout for the recreation room and Gwenda Watkins, the social director. She slowed her steps. If she didn't find them, she could leave. No one would blame her.

She found both in the Shangri-la wing.

"Come on in, Arabelle," Gwenda called. "We're having our juice and cracker break. Folks, say hello to Arabelle. Give her a wave."

"Help me! Help me!" The man from the torture chamber waved to her.

"That's Mr. Wexler, Arabelle."

"Yes, I know."

"Oh look, Mr. Rosen's waving." Gwenda lowered her voice. "Once in a while he forgets his clothes, Arabelle. You mustn't mind."

"I won't," she said, hiding her dismay.

"Give Mr. Huckabee a wave, Arabelle. Over there in the wheelchair. He's hard of hearing so you'll have to speak up."

"We've already met." She was introduced to everyone in the room and waved at by some. They all stared at her, except Mrs. Cushman, whose eyes were fixed on a spot invisible to the rest of them.

Arabelle dug deep for a smile that would disguise her disgust and dread — disgust as the sight of juice and crackers smooshed together on feeding trays and dribbling down chins, dread over the moment when Mr. Rosen would turn up without his clothes.

"Join us for juice and a cracker, Arabelle," Gwenda said. "There's plenty to go around."

Still smiling, Arabelle said, "That's okay, I'm not hungry. What would you like me to do?" She tried to put as much enthusiasm as possible into her voice. What she wanted was to fly from these human wrecks propped like laundry in their wheelchairs, close her ears to their mumbled gibberish, leave the smell of disinfectant behind her forever. Just one more week, and I'll be history, she promised herself.

"Sit with Mrs. Cushman for sing-along," Gwenda said. "See if you can get her to join in. She used to be very musical before she went downhill, if you know what I mean."

Gwenda must think she was born yesterday. "Doesn't she have — Alzheimer's?" Arabelle mouthed the word so Mrs. Cushman wouldn't hear.

"She sure does, Arabelle. But Happy believes there's still a part of her that hasn't gone to sleep. Isn't that a lovely way of putting it? We're hoping that with a little one-on-one, the dozing part will wake."

She accepted the songbook from Gwenda and pulled up a chair next to Mrs. Cushman. The first song was "Oh, What a Beautiful Morning," which they all seemed to know by heart. Mr. Wexler beat time with his foot and sang, "Help me, help me." Arabelle held the songbook up so Mrs. Cushman could see the words. Not that that was a problem.

"Where you going, Mr. Wexler?" Gwenda cried. They had just begun "The Bear Went Over The Mountain" when Mr. Wexler headed for the door.

"Help me! Help me!" he called over his shoulder and disappeared into the corridor.

Waving her hand in time to the music, Gwenda

beckoned to Arabelle. "Would you go see what Mr. Wexler's up to? We don't want him to wander off. We're a little short of staff today, otherwise I wouldn't ask you."

"I don't mind," Arabelle said, which wasn't entirely true. Though she hated where she was, she felt far safer under Gwenda's watchful eye than roaming the halls alone and unprotected.

She laid the songbook in Mrs. Cushman's lap and headed for the nurses' station. Not a soul around. Maybe Mr. Wexler was in his room. She trotted down the Aloha corridor. His door was open, but he wasn't there. Could he have wandered into the wrong room? She checked the rooms with open doors, careful not to go in. No sign of him.

"Mrs. Becker, have you seen Mr. Wexler?" Camille Becker, in elf-green tights and a leather vest, was on her way to the rec room.

"Not lately, dahling. I've just had a manicure and my roots touched up." She held out blood-red talons for Arabelle's inspection. "Is Mr. Wexler missing?"

"We're not sure. Gwenda's worried."

"Don't tell me," Mrs. Becker said. "Gwenda started the group singing the Bear song, and Mr. Wexler took off. Always happens. I don't know why she insists on that song."

"I'm supposed to find him and bring him back, Mrs. Becker. He's not in his room."

"Check outside. That's where he goes, if he can get through the doors without being caught."

"Omigosh!" Arabelle pictured him miles away, lost and confused, unable to tell anyone his name and address. "I'd better let Happy know. Where can I find her, Mrs. Becker?"

"Maybe in her office. But she's hardly ever there." Mrs. Becker frowned at her nails. "I think they're not red enough. What do you think?"

"Gwenda's counting on me, Mrs. Becker. What if something happens to him?" He might cross the street without looking and blunder into traffic, or collide with a speeding bicycle. A million catastrophes raced through her mind.

"You're hyperventilating, child. Mr. Wexler never goes far. See if you can catch him. I'll let Happy know he's escaped."

"Tell her it's an emergency." After a brief search, Arabelle found the button that opened the double doors. Apparently Mr. Wexler knew right where it was.

Mrs. Becker, pushing her walker ahead of her, called over her shoulder, "Did I miss juice and crackers?"

"You can have mine," Arabelle said. "I'm not hungry." In fact she felt quite ill. And she resented the heavy responsibility of a missing person laid on her because Heavenly Rest was short of staff. If she ran this place every inmate would be personally supervised, and doors guarded day and night. "The Bear Went Over The Mountain" would be permanently banned.

Arabelle rushed outside. Mr. Wexler couldn't have gone far, not in so short a time.

If I were Mr. Wexler, where would I go? she asked herself. Answer: I'd go home and never come back. Better check the highway, before he thumbs a ride or, worse, sits down in the middle of the road.

And that's as far as she got, because she spotted shoes by the reflecting pool — a man's shoes, and farther away a white sock. She picked them up. A second sock lay under a rhododendron bush between the Aloha wing and the Shangri-la wing, and beyond the rhododendron, the elusive Mr. Wexler sat in the grass, with his back to her, his legs extended and bare toes sticking out.

"Mr. Wexler, you shouldn't be out here. Come inside at once." He didn't move a muscle or signal in any way that he heard her.

"Right this minute, Mr. Wexler!" she cried, vexed at being ignored, mad for having worried and chased after him, and madder still that she'd delayed picking a volunteer activity from Mrs. Peeples' approved list while she had the chance. What in the world was so interesting that Mr. Wexler ignored her?

Birds, she discovered. Mr. Wexler was feeding the birds. Six sparrows hopped on and off his legs and pecked at crumbs in the grass. A chickadee joined them and was driven off. Very slowly, Mr. Wexler reached a hand into his pocket and took out a piece of cracker, which he crumbled in his fingers. The sparrows, heads cocked, watched and waited. Mr. Wexler laid his hand, palm up, on the ground.

Arabelle held her breath. It was impossible to feel angry or disgusted when someone fed small birds, even an old someone like Mr. Wexler who constantly asked for help.

Two of the greedier sparrows took turns eating out of Mr. Wexler's hand. Another sparrow lit on Mr. Wexler's toes. With his free hand, he reached into his other pocket. Out came a folded napkin and a few more crumbs. The chickadee returned.

Very carefully, so she wouldn't scatter the birds, Arabelle knelt beside Mr. Wexler. Man and beast ignored her. No bird had ever eaten from her hand, or come close, however hard she tried. It was a matter of trust, her father said.

Too soon the crumbs were gone, every last crumb in Mr. Wexler's palm and in the grass devoured. He turned out both his pockets. Mr. Wexler was fresh out of crumbs. The chickadee took off, but the sparrows stuck around.

Mr. Wexler looked at her. "Help me! Help me!"

"I don't have a cracker, Mr. Wexler. I'm really sorry. Do you think we can go inside now? Maybe after you put your shoes and socks on?" His toes worried her. Long white toes should be covered. She handed him his socks, one at a time, then his shoes. The sparrows gave up.

"Help me! Help me!" he said.

Arabelle had no idea what he wanted until he held up his hands. She pulled him to his feet and steadied him. For a grown man, he didn't weigh very much. His hands were warm and dry. Slowly, with her arm around his waist, they reached the front door.

They collided with Happy in the doorway. "Glory be!

Arabelle, you're an angel of mercy. Mr. Wexler, you are a lucky man."

"He was feeding the birds, weren't you, Mr. Wexler?"

"Help me! Help me!"

"What are we to do with you, Mr. Wexler?" Happy chided. "We worry when you run off and don't tell us where you're going." She took Mr. Wexler's hand in hers. "You don't want us to worry, now do you?"

"Help me! Help me!"

"Shall I take him back to the rec room, Happy?" Arabelle shrank at the thought. She wished they could stay outside. It was better feeding the sparrows.

"Mr. Wexler, do you want to bat-the-ball with Gwenda or take a little nap?"

"Help me! Help me!"

"He wants to take a nap, Arabelle."

"How can you tell?"

Happy smiled at her puzzlement. "I just can. If you listen very closely you'll detect slight variations in his calls for help. I've trained my ear, you see."

"Help me! Help me!"

"What's he saying now, Happy?"

"I can't always tell. Let's walk Mr. Wexler to his room."

Mr. Wexler gave Arabelle his hand like a trusting child. It was still warm and dry, the thin fingers surprisingly strong.

"I'll take over, Miss Happy." A nurse shooed them off and steered Mr. Wexler down the hall. To Arabelle's ears, his cries for help sounded the same as before. Her untrained ear had a long way to go.

"Does he ever say anything else, Happy?"

"Not since his wife died, Arabelle." Happy lowered her voice. "It's a sad, sad story. Apparently the Wexlers were hiking the Old Forge Trail —"

"I know that trail. It's not far from here."

Happy nodded. "Mrs. Wexler collapsed with a heart attack. No one was around to help. When they were finally found, Mrs. Wexler had passed on and Mr. Wexler was beside himself. All he could say was 'Help me.' Since he's been with us, that's all he ever says."

"That's so terrible. Poor Mr. Wexler!" No wonder he was reduced to cries for help. She tried to imagine going through life using two words and what those words would be. "He took his shoes and socks off, Happy."

"He always does when he's outside. You see, he and Mrs. Wexler were barefoot when they were found. They'd been wading in a brook nearby. It was a hot day." Happy sighed. "They were a devoted couple, Arabelle."

"Do you think he'll ever say anything besides 'Help me'?"

"Dr. Mosher, our house physician, says it's very unlikely. But we'll keep trying. We never give up hope at Heavenly Rest."

Arabelle did not return to the rec room. Happy said she'd done more than enough. Rescuing Mr. Wexler was a taxing experience, especially for a volunteer on her very first day, and anyway it was almost time for lunch and folks would be lining up soon outside the dining room.

"We'll see you next Saturday, Arabelle. We will see you, won't we?"

"I guess so." A cloud passed over Happy's face. "I'll be here," Arabelle said, ashamed for causing a cloudy day. One more Saturday and she could turn her back on Heavenly Rest forever, never have to hold the songbook for Mrs. Cushman, never have to squeeze her eyes shut when she met Mr. Rosen in the hallway, never have to humor Mr. Huckabee when he called her Clarabelle and asked why she was smiling.

However, brushing aside thoughts of Heavenly Rest proved impossible. On her ride home, the vision of Mrs. Wexler dying by the side of a stream and Mr. Wexler crying out for help pursued her like a specter. Something must be done. Mr. Wexler couldn't just be left to languish with only two words at his disposal. Arabelle consulted her heart. At times like this, her heart rarely failed her. Next Saturday, she'd work one-on-one with Mr. Wexler. They'd feed the birds together, and by lunchtime he'd be chatting up a storm. Dr. Mosher gave up too easily.

She'd start Mr. Wexler on simple words like yes and no, then introduce kelp and yelp, which should be easy for him because they rhymed with help. Happy would be thrilled. Dr. Mosher would shake his head and say, "Who's responsible for this medical miracle?" and Happy would say, "Our volunteer high schooler who's in ninth grade and truly amazing." But the happiest person of all would be Mr. Wexler. "You're my guardian angel," he'd tell her and she'd reply, "I knew you could do it. I never doubted it for a moment." As her father said, it was a matter of trust.

Act One

Arabelle had to wait until Monday to sound off about Heavenly Rest. Erna Sue was in St. Louis at a debutante party for her cousin, and Boris was on a two-day field trip with other Rotary scholars.

On her way to school Arabelle prepared for a possible encounter with Jeff Anderson, in case he noticed her.

He was still at his locker when she arrived. "Yo, Shorty! How's life so low to the ground?"

He was testing her. She sorted quickly through snappy comebacks. "Massively awesome, Jeff. I didn't know you were bowlegged." This always worked, no matter whom it was said to.

"What?" Jeff looked down. "Hey, my legs are straighter than yours, runt."

"You see things when you're short. Bet I could throw

a refrigerator between your legs. Must be from all that hockey."

"Five bucks you can't slide a sheet of paper between my knees. Come on." Jeff waved his math homework at her.

Arabelle smiled. "There's corrective surgery for bow-legs, Jeff. You don't need to go through life disadvantaged." She shut her locker door and took off fast before he could zing her back and win.

In truth, his legs were as straight as hers. But she figured that if you were tall and broad-shouldered and had hazel eyes, a mane of tawny hair, and a lazy smile that she swore he practiced in the mirror, you needed an occasional reminder that you weren't perfect. Deirdre would have cheered her on.

At noon, after the slowest morning on record, Arabelle was first through the lunch line. Erna Sue and Boris set their trays down across from her. At last she could vent about Heavenly Rest, except that since Saturday her experience at Heavenly Rest had grown less terrible.

She had barely started when Erna Sue interrupted. "Your experience can't have been worse than mine, Alex. I suffered debutantes for two days. I heard all about their boyfriends and what they do with their boyfriends and the cotillion in December that *Vogue* is dedicating eight whole pages to."

"Please, what is vogue?"

"It's a fashion magazine," Erna Sue said, "filled with eight-foot models who weigh ninety pounds."

"Can I please tell you guys about Heavenly Rest?"

"Da! Go for it." Boris grinned at Erna Sue. "Did I say right?"

"Yes, you did, Boris. Go ahead, Alex. Tell us what happened."

Her tale was heavily invested with "wait'll you hear this," and "how disgusting is that!" She was far milder when she told them about Mrs. Cushman and how she sat and stared and didn't speak. Mr. Wexler sparked the most discussion after she told his story.

"Everyone should learn CPR," Erna Sue said. "You never know when you'll be called on to save a life. If Mr. Wexler had known CPR, Mrs. Wexler would be alive and well."

"How you know?" Boris challenged. "Maybe time to die, maybe in stars."

"How DO you know. Dying has nothing to do with stars. Dying happens when no one's around to help."

Arabelle quickly changed the subject before an argument started. Boris's English wasn't up to arguments and she had no wish to debate Erna Sue, who made a habit of never being wrong.

"Mrs. Cushman used to be musical," she told them. "Happy hopes that sing-along will strike some chord deep within her."

Erna Sue shook her head. "Don't you realize what Alzheimer's does to the brain, Alex? Fibers and plaque collect in the cerebral cortex and hippocampus, which causes the brain to deteriorate. As time goes by more and more cells die until all a person can do is sit and stare."

Arabelle stopped listening. She had heard enough, and by the confused look on his face, so had Boris. "Do you suppose music plays in Mrs. Cushman's head?" she asked him.

"Da. We find chord inside her. I bring balalaika, sing folk songs my babushka — baba — how you say?"

"Grandma," Erna Sue murmured.

"— my grandma teach me."

"You mean that?" Arabelle asked, touched by his offer to serenade Mrs. Cushman, and on a Saturday morning.

"Da."

"I hate to break the news, people, but according to science, you're wasting your time."

"And just maybe science is wrong," Arabelle fired back. Usually she let Erna Sue have the last word.

With a shrug Erna Sue gathered up her tray and headed for the door.

Arabelle frowned over the remains of her ravioli. Would it kill Erna Sue to keep an open mind just once? Anything was possible if you believed long enough and hard enough. Like going to the moon. Or playing Essie Carmichael in the school play.

That afternoon at rehearsal, while the cast looked on from the front row seats, Arabelle helped Mr. Zee drag a table and chairs to center stage. The dining room table was where the Sycamore family ate and where a lot of the action took place. Behind the table loomed an old-fashioned sideboard, the largest piece of furniture on stage. To the right of the sideboard, a doorway hung with drapes opened to reveal the front hall and staircase.

"This is how most of you will get on and off the stage," Mr. Zee said. "Stairs are being built."

On the right side of the stage, Mr. Zee had set up a rickety card table with an old-fashioned typewriter on top. This was where Grandpa's daughter Penelope wrote her unfinished plays. Across stage there was a couch, and behind it, a cardboard box that served as a printing press until a real one could be found. Arabelle tried out the xylophone on loan from the school orchestra.

Mr. Zee took stock of the makeshift set and props. "Who's got the snakes?"

"Right here." Chip Wittington held a glass tank aloft. "They're my little brother's."

"Omigod, snakes!" Bonnie squealed. "I can't be on stage with snakes. I'll faint. What if they get loose?"

"They won't. But if you want to quit, I'll understand."

"I didn't mean that, Mr. Zee. Can't the snakes be fake? How many of us want fake snakes?"

"The snakes stay."

"They're garter snakes," Chip said, "and perfectly harmless. Let me take one out —"

"Don't you dare!" Bonnie screeched. "I can't stand snakes!"

"Enough!" Mr. Zee cried. "I will not tolerate hysterics. I'm the only one allowed hysterics!" The snake tank was placed on the sideboard.

With a sigh Arabelle took her seat in the wings and opened her playbook. What she wouldn't give to be on stage, acting her heart out and fulfilling her destiny. She'd walk on snakes if that's what it took.

"Okay, let's get into character," Mr. Zee said. "In the first act we meet the Sycamore family, presided over by Grandpa. Grandpa's idea of a good time is collecting snakes and going to college commencements. His daughter Penelope writes bad plays that she never finishes and her husband Paul makes fireworks in the cellar for July 4th celebrations. Their daughter Essie dances around the house all day in a tutu. She dreams of becoming a great ballerina, but Kolenkhov, her ballet instructor, thinks she's terrible. Essie's husband Ed prints 'Dynamite the Government' leaflets for fun, which he circulates in candy boxes. The only normal one in the family is Alice Sycamore, Paul and Penelope's daughter. Alice and Tony Kirby are in love and want to get married."

Mr. Zee looked around at his actors. "*Joie de vivre* is what the Sycamores are all about. Unabashed joy in the simple life and having fun, despite the world's disapproval. Is everyone clear?"

Heads nodded.

"Good. Kyra, let's start with Essie's entrance in act one, your scene with Penelope. Where's Penelope?"

"She went to the Nurse's Office with cramps," Kyra said.

"*Merde.* Come out here, Arabelle, and read Penelope's lines."

Her big chance! Cramps were often fatal. She bounded from the wings and plunked herself down in front of the typewriter. Penelope was working on her new play, *Sex Takes a Holiday*. Clutching the script, Arabelle waited breathlessly for Essie's opening line.

"'My, that kitchen's hot,'" Kyra said in her Essie voice, fanning herself and twirling on one toe.

In the lofty tones of a great actress, Arabelle replied, "'What, Essie?'" After deep, prolonged concentration, she typed a few words with her free hand.

"'I say the kitchen's awful hot.'" Essie twirled on her other toe. "'That new candy I'm making — it just won't ever get cool.'"

"'Do you have to make candy today, Essie? It's such a hot day.'" Arabelle waved a hand in front of her face to show she was stifling. Great actresses left nothing to chance.

"Arabelle, just say the lines straight," Mr. Zee said. "We're not handing out Oscars. Kyra, we don't want Swan Lake. Essie's supposed to be a lousy dancer, not Maria Tallchief."

"Hi, Mr. Zee. Sorry I'm late." The senior playing Penelope Sycamore stumbled up the stairs onto the stage.

"Don't be late again. Let's start over. Arabelle, go back to prompting."

Nonfatal cramps! Just her luck. How could she give the performance of her life when her best lines were still to come? "I don't mind reading longer, Mr. Zee. Are you sure you're okay?" she whispered to Penelope, whose real name she couldn't remember. "Maybe you should lie down."

"And have Mr. Zee replace me?" Penelope whispered back. "No way."

Mr. Zee's voice rumbled out of the darkness. "Arabelle, did you hear me?"

"I heard." Grumbling, she trudged off stage, one cramp away from proving herself a great actress.

Act one started over. At first no one forgot their lines, which was good because Arabelle, sunk in gloom, lost her place in the playbook. She found it just as Penelope began her speech to Ed and Essie:

"'Ed, dear. Why don't you and Essie have a baby?'" Penelope paused.

"'I was thinking about it just the other day,'" Arabelle prompted.

Penelope glared at her. "I didn't forget. I was pausing. Mr. Zee said to."

"I thought you forgot."

"Well, I didn't."

What the play needed was a mind reader. Arabelle wrote PAWS!!! after "baby" so she'd remember.

The scene continued to Grandpa's heart-to-heart with God:

"'Well, Sir, we're doing okay and want to thank you —'"

Arabelle broke in. "'Well, Sir, we've been getting along pretty good for quite a while now.' And then you say, 'We're certainly much obliged.'"

"That's what I said."

"No, you didn't. You left out 'getting along' and

'pretty good —'"

Mr. Zee interrupted, "What's going on?"

"She wants me to be word perfect," Grandpa said.

"The gist is good enough for now, Arabelle."

She doubted that the playwrights would agree. Gritting her teeth, she scrawled GIST!!! after Grandpa's speech.

"Let's move on to the love scene between Tony and Alice," Mr. Zee called. "End of act one."

Arabelle turned the page. If given half a chance, she could play Alice Sycamore without breaking a sweat. Instead, she was forced to watch Bonnie Atwood make out with Chip Wittington, the nicest guy in the senior class, possibly the entire school. Chip was like a big brother, if you were lucky enough to have one. Nice looking but not a hunk, serious but not overly so, respectful of everyone — including lowly prompters.

When Tony and Alice finally kissed, Arabelle noted with satisfaction that Chip didn't exactly put his heart into it. Bonnie's steamy kiss went far beyond what the moment required.

"Hold it!" Mr. Zee called. "Bonnie, who do you think you're kissing?"

"Tony, Mr. Zee. Alice and Tony are in love. They're supposed to kiss. Those are the directions —"

"I know what the directions are. Tony and Alice are a couple of nice square kids. They are not lovers in a bodice ripper. Take your lead from Chip, Bonnie. Kiss him the way he kisses you."

"But don't you think that a passionate kiss instead of

the way Chip kisses is more up-to-date? The audience will expect a modern kiss. We don't want to disappoint them." Chip gazed at Bonnie, his arms folded. "Bonnie, let Mr. Zee direct. Okay?"

"I am, Chippy darling. Mr. Zee values my insights as an actress, don't you, Mr. Zee?"

"I could do with fewer insights and more performance."

Bonnie laughed her tinkly laugh, but under her breath she said, "Crank!"

She and Chip did the scene over. This time Chip's kiss was less offhand and Bonnie controlled herself.

"I want to go back to Kolenkhov's entrance," Mr. Zee said. "Boris, you need to be much louder. Kolenkhov is a bear of a man, very loud, very Russian. When you appear for the first time in the doorway and say, 'Good evening, everybody!' you want the audience in the palm of your hand."

Boris grinned. "Won't fit in palm." Everyone laughed, Bonnie the loudest. Arabelle was amazed that he understood the expression well enough to joke.

Boris's second try was perfect. How he could stand on stage and appear twice his normal size, with a booming voice that suggested huge hairy arms and tons of chest hair, was nothing short of a miracle.

Mr. Zee's voice erupted from the darkness. "Much better, Boris. Essie, after Kolenkhov throws his hat on the sideboard and you say 'I practiced today, Mr. Kolenkhov,' I want you to do a grand jeté."

"No problem, Mr. Zee." Breaking into a run, Kyra leapt high in the air and somersaulted on her way down. "How was that?" she asked, steadying herself after narrowly missing the dining room table.

"No somersaults! Essie's a ballet dancer, not an acrobat."

Shielding her eyes, Bonnie peered into the darkened auditorium. "Kyra's a gymnast, Mr. Zee. Won't the audience expect at least one somersault? What about Kyra's coach?"

"What about him?"

"He'll expect a somersault if he's in the audience, won't he, Kyra?"

"For sure. He likes me to display my talent whenever I can. Just one, Mr. Zee, please?"

"Absolutely not. I forbid it."

"Can we vote, Mr. Zee?" Bonnie asked.

"No, we can't!"

The scene continued and for the first time Bonnie forgot her lines. "La, la, la, something, something," she chanted.

Arabelle leaned forward. At last, a chance to shine. "'Well, if you'll excuse us, Mr. Kolenkhov —'"

Bonnie ignored her. "La, la, la, I wonder what I say next."

Mr. Zee chased down the aisle. "You forget your line, you wait for the prompt."

"She didn't give it to me."

Arabelle darted from the wings. "Yes, I did, loud

and clear."

"Well, I didn't hear it. Sorry, Alex." Bonnie smiled and tugged her left earlobe.

"You didn't hear me on purpose."

Mr. Zee took Arabelle by the arm and walked her off stage. "Don't let your voice drop. A prompter's job is to be heard."

"If I prompt any louder, I'll be heard in China."

"Arabelle, slow down. You're trying too hard."

Another brick wall! She was only doing her job. How could she be the best prompter James Madison ever had if she didn't try her hardest?

At the end of act one the cast gathered on stage for Mr. Zee's comments. Erna Sue sat by his side, her notepad open.

"Why aren't you dancing on your toes, Kyra? You said you dance ballet."

"In gymnastics you dance on the balls of your feet, Mr. Zee."

"This isn't gymnastics. I want you on your toes. Chip, you need to project your voice. I couldn't always hear you. Bonnie, please play Alice straight. Goo-goo eyes and tossing your hair are wrong for Alice."

Mr. Zee glanced at Erna Sue's notes. "Grandpa, after your first entrance, when you say 'You don't know how lucky you are you're snakes,' I don't want you to stare into space. The snakes will not be in space. They'll be in Chip's younger brother's aquarium, on the sideboard behind the dining room table. That's where you should look."

The critique continued until the actors knew exactly what Mr. Zee wanted.

"We'll do the first act again tomorrow and for the rest of the week," he announced. "No excuses for lateness or not knowing your lines."

Riding home on the bus, Arabelle cheered herself up by daydreaming about the school play. If she were Deirdre, she'd have the lead role by now. From the moment she set foot on a London stage, Deirdre was destined for greatness:

... The velvet curtains slowly parted to reveal a stooped figure shrouded in black. Her slender arms outstretched, Deirdre Glendenning wept bitter tears over an open grave. "Prithee, take me with you, husband. I cannot live without you. My life has lost all meaning." Some in the audience broke out crying and were instantly shushed. No one wanted to miss a word spoken by this brilliant actress who had appeared overnight, from out of nowhere ...

Lost in a reverie, Arabelle almost missed her stop. The driver had to yell at her.

Lovely Young Man

Saturday morning Arabelle woke with a start. Boris had promised to show up at Heavenly Rest and play the balalaika. She worried that the inmates might act out and wondered what Boris would think. She worried about Mr. Rosen most of all.

"What's going on?" her father asked as she stomped on a bag of saltines in the kitchen.

"It's for Mr. Wexler, Daddy. I told you and Mom about him. He feeds the birds and says 'Help me.'"

"You'll do better with birdseed." Mr. Archer rummaged in the pantry for his special mix of seed and pine nuts.

"We're feeding sparrows, Daddy. Sparrows eat anything."

"You'll attract more than sparrows if you offer seed."

"Yeah, like squirrels and raccoons."

Her father smiled patiently. "I had finches and nuthatches in mind. Maybe a passing condor or two."

Of course he was joking. She couldn't always tell. Whatever came out of his mouth sounded the same.

Her mother stopped her at the front door. "Can I run you out to Heavenly Rest, sweetie?"

"No, thanks. I'll take my bike."

"Three miles is a bit of a haul. You're getting off a little later than last week."

"Mom! There's plenty of time. You don't need to check on me."

Mrs. Archer sighed. "I'm not, Arabelle. I think you're terrific to volunteer at Heavenly Rest and if a ride is welcome, I'm glad to provide one."

"I'm sorry, it's just that I'm not terrific, because I haven't done anything. Not one thing! And I don't want to go to Heavenly Rest, but Mr. Wexler won't start talking unless I do." He was counting on her. So was Happy and so was Dr. Mosher. She mustn't fail them.

Ashamed of her outburst, Arabelle grabbed her bike and headed for the highway. She was on her own. Even Deirdre couldn't help her with this.

Happy was at the reception desk when she swung through the front door.

"You're here! I hoped you'd come."

"I said I would, Happy."

"Of course. But saying is one thing, doing quite another."

Arabelle noticed how shrewd Happy's eyes were when they weren't crinkled up from smiling. "I brought birdseed from home. I thought Mr. Wexler and I could feed the sparrows."

"What bliss! Let's tell him together."

Armchair aerobics were in full swing. Arabelle hung back out of sight so the residents wouldn't see her and wave hello and make her feel awful for avoiding them.

"Arabelle's going to borrow Mr. Wexler for a bit, Gwenda. She'll return him safe and sound."

Happy rescued Mr. Wexler from Gwenda's flexing exercises and led him into the hall. At the sight of Arabelle, his face lit up.

"Hi, Mr. Wexler. I thought we could feed the birds." She held up the bag of birdseed, unsure how much he understood.

"He knows what you're saying, Arabelle. Don't you, Mr. Wexler?"

"Help me! Help me!"

"He said 'yes,' didn't he, Happy?"

"Your ear is catching on. Soon you and Mr. Wexler will be chatting away like old friends."

Arabelle took Mr. Wexler's hand and headed for the front door. By noon she'd have him talking a blue streak.

"Don't keep him out too long," Happy called. "He tires easily."

"Oh, I almost forgot," Arabelle said. "A friend of mine from school is meeting me here. He's from Ukraine. If it's okay with you and Gwenda, he'd like to play folk songs on his balalaika for the inma — residents. I told him about Mrs. Cushman being musical."

Happy beamed. "What a gift from heaven you are. I'll let Gwenda know."

Once they were outside, Mr. Wexler took off his shoes and socks and made straight for the reflecting pool. Arabelle trotted after him.

"This way, Mr. Wexler." She grabbed hold of his sleeve. "The birds are this way, behind the rhododendrons, remember?"

"Help me! Help me!"

She tugged his sleeve harder, then pulled his arm. But he was not to be turned from his course, nor persuaded by the bag of birdseed that she waved in front of his nose.

"Please, Mr. Wexler. We can visit the reflecting pool some other day." Pleading did no good. "I'm responsible for you, Mr. Wexler. I don't want to get into trouble."

Mr. Wexler sat at the edge of the pool and rolled his trousers up. Arabelle looked on in dismay as he dipped one foot in the water, then the other. "Help me! Help me!"

"I can't if you don't say how. Do you want to go back inside?" She was pretty sure he didn't.

"Help me! Help me!"

"Try to say yes or no, Mr. Wexler."

Before she could stop him, he slipped into the water and waded to the middle of the pool. The bottoms of his trousers were quite wet.

"Come back, Mr. Wexler." She kicked off her shoes and charged after him, spraying water in all directions.

"Stop! Come back!"

A second later he swung around and splashed her. It was no accident. He had splashed her on purpose. This was more than she'd bargained for. When she met behavior like this, she was usually babysitting and got paid. Enough was enough. Time to get him out of the pool, dried off, and back to Gwenda. The birds could fend for themselves.

She lunged for him, but her foot slipped and the next moment she was sitting in waist-high water. Mr. Wexler chuckled and sat down in the water facing her.

"Help me! Help me!" He splashed her again. Small, friendly splashes, more on the order of wavelets. Then, a tsunami.

"Mr. Wexler, plea —"

"Help me! Help me!" His eyes danced. He was daring her.

Well, okay, if that's what he wanted. She splashed him back and he splashed her and she splashed him and instead of taking turns they splashed each other at the same time.

"Help me! Help me!"

Another tsunami hit her. And another. Laughing, she scrambled to her knees and with both hands flung water at Mr. Wexler.

He ducked. "Help me!"

"Please, here is Boris!" Boris Petrenko stood by the side of the pool, peering at them with a quizzical smile, his balalaika slung over one shoulder.

Arabelle struggled to her feet. He had caught her frisking like a seal. She'd never live this down. "Quick, help me get Mr. Wexler out of the pool."

"Da. He sure wet. You, too."

"I had to rescue him," she huffed, galled by her silly behavior and, worse, that she had enjoyed herself. "Come on, Mr. Wexler, time to go inside and dry off."

She led him willingly to Boris's outstretched hands and together they hauled him out of the pool. "Don't put your socks on, Mr. Wexler. You're too wet. We'll go barefoot." She dreaded what Happy would say.

They trailed water all the way to the Aloha corridor. Boris carried their shoes and socks.

"Mercy, a pair of drowned rats." Happy's eyes widened at the spectacle.

"I'm sorry about this, Happy. Mr. Wexler got into the pool before I could stop him. I should have taken better care of him."

"Water never hurt anyone, Arabelle. Mr. Wexler probably had the time of his life. Did you, Mr. Wexler?"

"Help me! Help me!"

"There, you see?"

Arabelle took his hand. "Can you say yes? Just this once? Just for me?"

Mr. Wexler covered her hand with his. "Help me, help me," he said softly.

She waited in vain for a miracle that seemed less likely with each passing moment. Her hopes had come to nothing, absolutely nothing. Somehow she had to find a way.

"Never mind," Happy said. "You and I know what he means. This must be your friend from Ukraine."

"Please, I am Boris. I play songs on balalaika."

"What a treat! But first we need dry clothes for Arabelle and Mr. Wexler. Lana, take Mr. Wexler to his room and dry him off."

Arabelle recognized the nurse's aide from a week ago. Mr. Wexler was led away, protesting.

"Dry clothes, Mr. Wexler. Then join us in the rec room."

Happy showed Arabelle to the laundry. Her wet clothes went into the dryer. A nurse's aide jumpsuit, several sizes too big, replaced them. The waist hung below her hips. She rolled up the sleeves and the pant legs. Happy zipped her up the back.

Boris grinned when he saw her.

"Say one word, and I'll never speak to you again!" Arabelle wished he hadn't come. He had seen her at her worst. A volunteer worker shouldn't frolic in a pool or wear a jumpsuit if she hoped to be taken seriously.

Boris shrugged, but the grin stayed.

They followed Happy to the rec room where Mrs. Becker, in a scarlet caftan and matching turban, was reciting at the top of her voice. She stopped them with an imperious sweep of her arm. "Not one step farther 'til I've finished my soliloquy. Saint Joan is about to choose death over prison —"

"Get on with it!" Mr. Huckabee yelled. "You're taking forever!"

Mrs. Becker stared down her nose at him. "Great art must never be rushed. Where was I? Oh, yes."

Surrounded by wheelchairs and walkers, she brandished her red enameled finger like a sword. "'I could do without my warhorse. I could drag about in a skirt . . .'"

Happy, Arabelle, and Boris eased into the room as Saint Joan cast her eyes up to heaven. Mrs. Cushman stared into space, her mouth open.

"Mrs. Becker likes to entertain us," Happy whispered. "Last week she was Peter Pan."

As Saint Joan sucked in air for the final sprint to the stake, Mr. Rosen strolled through the door. "Good morning, my dears. How are we this morning? Camille, have I missed a performance?"

The room erupted in groans.

Arabelle almost fainted. Her worst nightmare had come true. Except for short argyle socks and black lace-up shoes, Mr. Rosen was stark naked. She didn't know where to look. Mr. Rosen's bald spot seemed the safest place, far away from everything below the neck.

"Not again!" Mr. Huckabee cried. "For God's sake, Rosen!"

Mrs. Becker cast a long-suffering look at Mr. Rosen as he circled the room greeting residents, a folded newspaper under his arm. "Haven't you forgotten something, Mr. Rosen?"

"Have I?" Puzzled, Mr. Rosen shook his head, then glanced down. "Oh, dear, so I have. Sorry, sorry. Forgive me."

Happy sailed after Mr. Rosen. "You're not dressed, Mr. Rosen. You know the rules as well as I."

"So sorry, so sorry." Mr. Rosen held the newspaper in front of himself.

Lana breezed through the door. "I got him, Miss Happy. Shame on you, Mr. Rosen! Folks don't want to see you in your birthday suit."

"Ordinarily I don't mind," Mrs. Becker sniffed, "but I will not be upstaged when I'm reciting."

Boris burst out laughing.

"It's not funny," Arabelle hissed, "Mr. Rosen should be arrested."

"Everyone crazy. Everyone have joy de veever. Like play at school."

She couldn't believe her ears. What was he talking about? The play and Heavenly Rest had nothing in common. Nothing.

"I'm so sorry," Happy said to Boris, after Lana led Mr. Rosen away. "We're usually better behaved than this. Mr. Rosen is our newest resident. He came to us from a nudist colony. Now and then he forgets to put his clothes on. I hope we haven't scared you to death."

"Is okay. I enjoy." Arabelle could tell by the size of his grin that he meant it.

Order was soon restored and Boris introduced. "This lovely young man is from Ukraine," Happy said, "and a friend of Arabelle's. He is going to play the balalaika for us and sing songs. Do join us, Mr. Wexler. You're just in time." Mr. Wexler stood in the doorway.

"Are they Commie songs?" Mr. Huckabee barked. "Songs about tractors and collective farms make me sick."

"Feel free to leave. You won't be missed," an old lady with a cane yelled.

Mr. Huckabee settled back in his wheelchair. He had no intention of leaving.

"I sing love song and gypsy song my babushka teach me."

"Are you going to sing to us in Russian?" Mrs. Becker asked.

"Da — yes."

"Do you mind if I close my eyes, lovely young man? When I'm sung to in Russian, I like to close my eyes and let my imagination take me where it will."

"I no mind. Maybe you end up prisoner of Cossack prince," Boris teased, "in tent, on Russian Steppe."

Mrs. Becker let out a tiny scream. "Is he young and gorgeous?"

"Da."

"Start singing before she takes over," Arabelle whispered.

Boris strummed a few notes on the balalaika. "This is gypsy song about two lovers. They no part themselves so can die together."

In a light baritone voice Boris sang several verses in a language no one understood or needed to, because when lovers die together, words aren't necessary. When he finished, he got a big round of applause.

"I didn't understand a damn word," Mr. Huckabee

grunted.

Mrs. Becker glared at him. "That's because you're dumb as a brick, you old goat."

"Enough with the kvetching," the old lady yelled. "We're sick of it."

"Mr. Wexler liked the song," Gwenda said before Mr. Huckabee kvetched back. "He'd like another, wouldn't you, Mr. Wexler?"

"Help me! Help me!"

"Sing Mrs. Cushman a song, Boris. She's over here." Arabelle didn't have to point her out. By the look of her, Boris knew who she was.

He stooped at her feet and strummed a few bars. "This folk song about gypsy horse thief." The song was lively and fast. Russian tripped off his tongue. With his hair tumbling over his brow, he was the wild gypsy he sang about.

By the end of the song, Mrs. Cushman's eyes were fastened on him. Without a pause Boris launched into another song, holding Mrs. Cushman's gaze with his own.

"You're getting through," Arabelle exclaimed, all goose bumps. "Mrs. Cushman blinked."

Mr. Huckabee snorted, "Big deal! Everyone blinks."

Happy laid her hand on his shoulder. "Please, Mr. Huckabee. When words fail, a blink speaks volumes. Mrs. Cushman is telling us what's in her heart, thanks to this lovely young man."

Arabelle almost burst, she was so proud of Boris and glad that he had come, despite her earlier qualms. Anything was possible as long as you held out hope, never stopped trying, kept on believing.

Boris strummed a new tune and sang softly, never once taking his eyes off Mrs. Cushman. She gazed back. In the distance the gong sounded for lunch, but no one in the room moved, lest they break the spell. The song ended on a note of sustained joy.

Mrs. Becker heaved a sigh. "How utterly divine. Lovely young man, you must come and sing to us often or we shall surely die."

Mr. Huckabee smirked at her. "You're going to anyway, you old bag!"

In a flash the spell that Boris had laid on Mrs. Cushman was sundered and she was back to staring.

Arabelle wanted to weep. Another setback! Boris had been so close. Now they'd have to start over. Then she remembered. This was her last week. She wasn't coming back. But how could she save Mr. Wexler from a life of two words if she stayed away? How could Boris coax a smile out of Mrs. Cushman if he stayed away? They had to come back. Shoulder to shoulder, they would bestow the gift of speech on Mr. Wexler and put a permanent smile on Mrs. Cushman's face.

Mrs. Becker stumped after them to the front door. "Goodbye, lovely young people, goodbye."

Boris clicked his heels together like Kolenkhov and kissed Mrs. Becker's outstretched fingers, which sent her into raptures.

"I will never wash this hand again." She stared spellbound at her kissed fingers.

In her rush out the door Arabelle forgot what she was wearing. Boris had to remind her that she might want to get her clothes out of the dryer and put them on before she went home.

Act Two

Jeff Anderson was waiting for her Monday morning. "Yo, Shorty! How's the air down there?"

Arabelle spun the dial on her locker. "Not too bad if you hold your nose."

"Why's that?" Jeff tried not to smile.

"So you don't asphyxiate from hockey socks."

"Arrgh! You really know how to hurt a guy. No kidding, how tall are you?"

"Two feet four," she quipped, deadpan.

He measured her with his eyes. "I'd say more like five feet. Maybe a little over."

"Hi, Jeff!" Kiki and the wraparounds slowed their steps. "Any new pics?"

He ignored them. "Got a boyfriend, Peanut?"

"Wouldn't you like to know!"

"Yeah, I would." Jeff leaned an elbow against his locker. She had his undivided attention.

Kiki shrugged. "See ya later, I guess."

"Well?" Jeff wanted an answer.

"You don't know him," Arabelle said, which was for sure, because neither did she.

"Try me."

"His name's Tim."

"Yeah? What's his last name?"

"Cratchit." She wondered if he'd get it.

Jeff laughed. "Tiny Tim. What a crazy girl. You crack me up, Shorty."

She basked briefly in the compliment before she made a narrow but triumphant escape. "See you!"

"Hey, wait —"

But she didn't. He would expect her to crack more jokes, and she was fresh out. Excited that the captain of the hockey team and the hottest guy in the junior class had noticed her for the second time in a week, Arabelle wondered if she could stretch one week to more.

"Maybe I'm the only funny girl he knows," she said to Erna Sue and Boris at lunch.

"It's more than that," Erna Sue said. "You're a challenge. You're his Mount Everest."

"I am?"

"It's simple psychology. You don't come on to him. You give him a hard time."

"But I make him laugh. That's not a hard time."

"It is if you tell him his socks smell and Tiny Tim's

your boyfriend."

"Jeff in love with Alex," Boris said. "He no care what she say."

Erna Sue scoffed at the idea. "The only person Jeff Anderson loves is Jeff Anderson. And, Boris, it's *he doesn't care what she says.*

"Not so loud," Arabelle hissed. The conversation had gone far enough. Too far, in her opinion.

Boris helped her describe their morning at Heavenly Rest. "Alex and Mr. Wexler have big water fight."

"What was that about?" Erna Sue asked.

Arabelle omitted some of the more embarrassing details.

"A perfect example of transference," Erna Sue said. "Mr. Wexler transferred his feelings for Mrs. Wexler to you, Alex. You became Mrs. Wexler. The Wexlers probably had a water fight the day she died."

"Happy said they were wading. She didn't mention a water fight."

"Of course she didn't, she wasn't there."

"How could I possibly be Mrs. Wexler? She must've been ancient."

"Age has nothing to do with transference."

"How you know — how DO you know this?" Boris asked.

"My cousin in St. Louis is in therapy. She's transferred her feelings twice."

Before Erna Sue could hold forth, Arabelle changed the subject. "Boris was a knockout. I wish you'd been there."

"Miz Cushman blink twice."

"Blinking is a reflex action, not a voluntary one," Erna Sue said.

Arabelle set her teeth. "Mrs. Cushman looked straight at Boris and blinked. Didn't she, Boris?"

"Da."

"And she almost smiled. If Mr. Huckabee hadn't ruined everything, she would have."

"Gas," Erna Sue said. "Old people have gas. It makes you smile."

"You weren't there," Arabelle snapped, "so how would you know?"

"Based on science —"

"Science once believed the sun circled the earth. How wrong was that?"

Erna Sue lifted her shoulders in an exaggerated shrug. "Believe what you want, Alex. People do, despite proof to the contrary."

Arabelle jumped up. "Boris and I saw what we saw, didn't we, Boris?"

"Da."

"And we intend to rouse Mrs. Cushman's inner self." She grabbed up her tray.

"I thought you were through with Heavenly Rest," Erna Sue said.

"Well, I'm not! And I intend to rescue Mrs. Cushman and prove *you* wrong!"

"Lots of luck, Alex."

"I don't need your luck! What I need is '*Go for it, Alex!
You can do it!*'"

Stung by Erna Sue's vote of no confidence, Arabelle
headed to the door. She had had enough. More than
enough. Was belief in a friend too much to ask? Apparently. If Erna Sue didn't believe in her, she'd find friends who
did. Once she succeeded with Mrs. Cushman and Erna
Sue admitted she was wrong, then — and only then —
would she forgive her.

At three o'clock sharp, Mr. Zee called the cast together.
Arabelle joined the actors on stage so she could hear what
he had to say. Erna Sue, armed with her notepad and flashlight, took her accustomed seat in the third row.

"She feel bad," Boris told Arabelle in a low voice.

"Well, so do I. I'm sick of being corrected." Until this
year, Erna Sue hadn't insisted on being right. Not all the
time. She'd corrected facts a little in seventh grade and a
little more in eighth, but not like now. Back then she was
hardly ever a pain.

"Is her nature. She no can help."

"She better try or she won't have any friends."

"Boris, Arabelle, you through?" Mr. Zee frowned them
into silence, then continued. "In the second act, everything goes wrong. Gay Wellington, a friend of Penelope's,
has one drink too many and passes out on the Sycamores'
couch. Alice is planning a dinner party to introduce her
family to the Kirbys, only Tony and his parents show up on
the wrong night and catch the Sycamores at their nuttiest.

In the course of the evening, Mr. Kirby gets mad at Mrs. Kirby over a silly game that Penelope insists on playing; and in despair, Alice quits her job at Mr. Kirby's Wall Street firm and breaks her engagement to Tony. To make matters worse, three G-men from the Justice Department burst in and arrest Ed Carmichael for printing "Down with the Government" fliers for fun, then discover explosives in the cellar. In the last scene, the cellar blows up and everyone goes to jail. Arabelle, I want you to cue up the explosions. I've marked the place in your playbook."

Mr. Zee rubbed the back of his neck. "Learned your lines yet, Bonnie?"

"Oh, Mr. Zee, you're so funny. Of course I have."

"Congratulations. Places, everyone. Gay, where's your whiskey bottle? Who's on props? Prop girl, where are you?"

"She's taking a make-up test," Erna Sue called.

Arabelle grabbed Gay's bottle and waved it. "I'll do props, Mr. Zee." She'd leap tall buildings to prove her worth.

The act began. Lizbeth Keppel, who played Gay Wellington, was a pretty good drunk. So good in fact that the other actors on stage started laughing and forgot to say their lines. To her credit, Lizbeth kept a perfectly straight face as she staggered around the set and passed out cold at the sight of Grandpa's snakes. By then everyone was in stitches.

"Stop right there," Mr. Zee yelled. "Unless I direct you to laugh, no one laughs. Even if the audience laughs."

The act continued to Alice's entrance. Bonnie crossed

the stage and threw her arms wide.

"'Oh, my darlings, I love you,'" she cried. "'You're the most wonderful family in the world and I'm the happiest —'"

Mr. Zee called out, "Bonnie, what are you doing?"

"I'm telling my family how much I love them. Shouldn't I be?"

"You should be telling them by the dining room table."

"I'll see the snakes if I stand there. You know how I feel about snakes."

"Bonnie, do you want to be in this play?"

"Yes, Mr. Zee. That's why I tried out."

"Good. Let's do the scene over. And try to get it right this time."

Bonnie did most of the scene with her eyes shut. Arabelle felt kind of sorry for her. Mr. Zee yelled at her a lot. Of course, she asked for it by arguing all the time.

Between prompting and subbing for the prop girl, Arabelle had her hands full. She was lining up darts for the next scene when Bonnie stopped in the middle of a speech.

"What's my line? Prompter, I need a line. Hello!"

"Just a sec." Arabelle looked around wildly. Where was her playbook? What had she done with it? Whew! There it was.

"Arabelle, are you with us?"

She poked her head around the curtain. "Sorry, Mr. Zee. I was at the prop table."

"This happens all the time, whenever we need a

prompt," Bonnie cried.

Arabelle darted from the wings. "This is the first time."

"She's not prompting me on purpose."

"That is so not true!" Arabelle glared at Bonnie across the dining room table.

"Quiet!" Mr. Zee yelled. "Arabelle, go back to prompting. Actors, you're responsible for your own props."

"I can manage both." Arabelle's voice trembled.

"You heard me," Mr. Zee said.

On her way by, Chip whispered, "You're doing great, Alex," which raised her spirits a little. The president of Student Council appreciated her.

The dance scene between Kolenkhov and Essie had begun when Mr. Zee stopped the action. "Boris, when Kolenkhov says to Essie 'We have a hot night for it, my Pavlova, but art is only achieved through perspiration,' I'd like you to take your shirt off."

"I no have chest hair, Mr. Zee."

"Chest hair doesn't matter. You okay about stripping?"

"I no mind." Boris unbuttoned his shirt as Chip Wittington hummed the song that strippers around the world take off their clothes to.

Arabelle couldn't think of one other person who'd do what Boris was doing. The reason was obvious once the shirt came off. Boris was built. In the pecs, abs, and delts department, he scored a perfect ten. Chip gave a wolf whistle and asked Boris for a date. Boris batted his eyes and accepted. Bonnie snapped a picture of him on her cell phone.

"Let's get going," Mr. Zee called. "Start from your opening line to Essie, Boris."

This dance lesson was a major scene, in which Kolenkhov instructed Essie at the top of his lungs while husband Ed accompanied her on the xylophone.

"'Pirouette! Come, come! You can do that!'" Kolenkhov roared. "'Entrechat! Entrechat!'" Taking two quick steps, Essie catapulted herself into an airborne flip.

"No! No! No!" Mr. Zee barreled down the aisle and onto the stage. "What did I tell you, Kyra? No somersaults! That goes double for flips!"

"I don't know what entrechat means," she wailed.

"It's explained in the directions. Come out here, Arabelle. Bring me the playbook."

Mr. Zee snatched it out of her hands and fished for his glasses, which weren't in his pocket. "Read the directions to Kyra, Arabelle."

"They're not real clear," she said, after reading them aloud. Somehow she survived Mr. Zee's glare.

"Who knows what an entrechat is?" he asked.

Erna Sue's voice rang out. "It's when a dancer jumps and crosses her legs several times in the air."

"Got that, Kyra?" Mr. Zee suddenly grabbed hold of his hair, his nose an inch from hers. "See this! Gray! Before its time! You know why? Because of actors who won't follow directions. Because of dancers who won't dance lousy."

"I'll do better, Mr. Zee — I mean worse."

"Let's hope so." Mr. Zee strode to the front of the

112

stage. "Okay, I want to do the scene right before the Kirbys' entrance. Essie, you're off to the side doing your dance lesson with Kolenkhov. Ed, you're playing music for them on the xylophone. Penelope, you're at your easel, in an artist's smock and beret, painting a portrait. Gay, you're still on the couch, passed out, with your behind sticking up. Grandpa?"

"Yes, Mr. Zee."

"During this scene you're shooting darts at your dart-board. Gay's behind is a tempting target. I want you to aim a dart at it, then change your mind. It's sure to get a laugh. No one in this scene looks or behaves normally. What Tony's folks see when they walk through the door is a display of complete nuttiness."

Bonnie fluttered her hand. "Wouldn't it be funnier if Grandpa aimed all his darts at Gay's behind? No offense, Lizbeth, but it is pretty big."

Lizbeth bared her fangs in a killer smile. "Almost as big as your mouth, Bonnie."

"One dart is funny," Mr. Zee said. "More than one is overkill." He trotted back to his seat.

The scene unfolded without a glitch. "Good," Mr. Zee called — the first "good" out of his mouth since rehearsals began. Kyra twirled in delight. Everyone relaxed as they prepared for the next scene, which was the sudden appearance of Tony and his parents on the wrong night and Alice's horror when she sees them.

"Come out, Arabelle," Mr. Zee yelled.

Oh, God, now what? She hadn't screwed up for

twenty minutes.

"I want you to sub for Mrs. Kirby. She had to leave early."

Had she heard him right? Maybe he had said something different than what she thought she heard. "I'm sorry?"

"Mrs. Kirby, Arabelle. You up to it?"

"Oh gosh, yes. Totally. I know some of her lines by heart —"

"Just read the script."

"Go for the gold, Alex," Arabelle told herself as she lined up with Tony and Mr. Kirby for their entrance. Like Deirdre, she would prove herself indispensable.

On cue, they stepped through the curtained doorway and waited for the Sycamores to gasp in horror and disbelief.

Then Bonnie entered. At the sight of the Kirbys, whom she spotted out of the corner of her eye because to look at them directly would have brought the snakes into her line of vision, she cried, "'Oh!'" her hand to her throat.

"'Darling, I'm the most dull-witted person in the world,'" Chip said in his Tony voice. "'I thought it was tonight.'"

Bonnie burst into tears. "'Why, Tony, I thought you — I'm so sorry —'" Her tears flowed and flowed. She had forgotten her next line.

"'Have you all met each other,'" Arabelle prompted.

"Bug off, Alex!"

"You're supposed to say 'Have you all met each other.'

We can't go on 'til you do."

Bonnie flounced to the front of the stage. "Mr. Zee, make her stop prompting me. I know my lines."

"I hadn't noticed. Wait for Bonnie to say her line, Arabelle."

"'Have you all met each other?'" Bonnie repeated, punching each word.

"'Yes, indeed,'" Mr. Kirby replied.

Silence. Arabelle quickly checked the playbook.

Bonnie's chest heaved with emotion. "'I'm afraid — I'm afraid —'"

"Line, Arabelle," Mr. Zee called.

"'I'm afraid I'm not very —'"

Bonnie glared at her. "'I'm afraid I'm not very something, something. I have such a fabulous new dress for our dinner and the most awesome menu planned for tomorrow night, but here you are on the wrong night, and I'm in shorts.'"

"That's not what you say," Arabelle whispered. "You wear a dress in this scene."

"Of course. Silly me!" Another glare.

"'Well, we'll come again tomorrow night,'" Mr. Kirby said.

"'There you are, Alice,'" Tony said. "'Am I forgiven?'"

Torn between forgiving him and strangling him, Alice stammered, "'I guess so. It's just that I — I —'" She sobbed into her hands.

Arabelle had to hand it to her. Sobbing filled a lot of dead air when you forgot your lines.

"Are you quite through?" Mr. Zee barked. "Because if you are, we will take the scene from the beginning, and you will speak the lines the playwrights have written and that Arabelle provides, and you will not clutch yourself, gasp, or sob. Am I clear?"

Bonnie peered at Mr. Zee three rows back. "But shouldn't Alice be played emotionally? Tony's parents have just had a close look at her crazy family. She's afraid Tony won't marry her."

"Did you hear what I just said?"

"Alice is majorly upset," Bonnie argued. "The audience needs to know that."

"Mr. Zee?" Kyra tripped to the front of the stage. "You're right that gasping and sobbing are a bit much, but couldn't Alice bite her lips and moan a little?"

The silence from the third row ticked like a time bomb.

"How many of us want me to break down in this scene?" Bonnie asked. "Show of hands."

Kyra's was the only hand raised, then quickly lowered.

Mr. Zee sprang to his feet. "*Merde!* I've had it! Direct yourselves!" He strode up the aisle and whirled around. "Better yet, let Bonnie direct you! It's all yours, Bonnie! Good luck!" And without another word or a backward glance, he slammed out of the auditorium.

"What'd I do?" Bonnie cried.

"Shut up, Bonnie," Chip snapped.

Every eye was trained on the door in back. Any minute now Mr. Zee would return. He had to.

But he didn't.

"Erna Sue, come on up here," Chip called. Erna Sue hurried down the aisle. "How mad is he?"

"Very mad. I don't think he'll come back."

"Then it's up to us to convince him," Chip said. "Any ideas?"

"Why don't we apologize?" Arabelle said. Her chance to be the best prompter James Madison ever had depended on getting Mr. Zee back.

"One of us, in particular, needs to apologize." Chip's eyes settled on Bonnie.

"Who, me?" she squealed. "I didn't do anything. I mean, if Mr. Zee can't stand a few suggestions — where are you taking me, Chippy?"

Gripping Bonnie by the arm, Chip propelled her to a far corner of the auditorium and sat her down. His voice was too low to be overheard but Bonnie's protests came through loud and clear: "No way! You can't make me, Chip Wittington! I'll quit!"

"If Bonnie quits, we'll need an understudy," Arabelle said, panic-stricken.

Lizbeth snorted. "Bonnie's a showboater, Alex. She'll never quit." Heads nodded in agreement but worried glances were exchanged.

Arabelle wanted to believe Lizbeth, but how could she — or any of them, for that matter — be sure?

"Mr. Zee doesn't use understudies," Erna Sue said. She hadn't looked at Arabelle once.

"How you know?" Boris asked.

"He told me."

Their fate in the balance, the cast watched Bonnie and Chip leave the auditorium together. Then, one by one, they collected their backpacks and jackets and straggled up the aisle and out the door.

Arabelle, fearing the worst, hung around backstage until she saw Erna Sue leave.

On Opposite Shores

Word got around the next day that Chip had marched
Bonnie to Mr. Zee's office, where the three of them met
behind closed doors. Afterwards Chip wouldn't speak
about the meeting and neither would Bonnie.

At noon Arabelle headed to the cafeteria. Boris and
Erna Sue sat across from each other at their usual table.
Arabelle hesitated, torn between joining them and staying
away. She didn't want to be mad at Erna Sue any longer.
But that meant apologizing, which she had no intention
of doing. It was up to Erna Sue to apologize.

Students in AP French occupied a table close by.
Arabelle joined them, and for thirty excruciating minutes
smiled and laughed and pretended to understand their
rapid-fire French. More than once she caught Erna Sue's
eyes on her.

Between World History and study hall she ran into Chip. "Is the play cancelled or are we rehearsing?"

"Don't know yet, Alex. Check the bulletin board for announcements."

It was almost three when she checked the board one last time.

CAST MEETING TODAY
3:00
BE ON TIME!!!

Arabelle hurried to the auditorium. The cast had already assembled on stage. Bonnie sat among them, talking a blue streak and laughing loudly. The play was on.

Giddy with relief, Arabelle marched straight up to her and said, "I — I'm glad you're here."

Bonnie looked her up and down. "Where else would I be, Alex?"

"I — we didn't want you to quit." Arabelle packed every ounce of sincerity into her smile.

"Well, thank you, Alex. I'm glad I'm here, too."

Arabelle ignored the sarcasm. Like Deirdre, she would take the high road and go the extra mile.

"Where Mr. Zee?" Boris asked. "Is play kaput?"

"We'll give him five more minutes . . ." Chip didn't finish his thought. He didn't have to.

At ten past three, Mr. Zee walked through the door and trudged down the aisle. Chip leapt to his feet. "Let's give Mr. Zee a hand," he said, and started clapping.

Arabelle joined Chip, and soon everyone was clapping. Without a word, Mr. Zee sat down in the front row.

Chip spoke for all of them. "Mr. Zee, we've been pretty hard on you the last few weeks. We hope you'll give us another chance. You won't regret it, I promise."

Arabelle marveled at Chip's apology, offered without excuses or finger-pointing. No wonder Chip Wittington was president of Student Council.

"Apology accepted, Mr. Wittington." Mr. Zee looked in turn at each of his actors, Bonnie the longest. "Let's get to work. Act two from the beginning, please."

For the rest of the week, between classes and at rehearsal, Arabelle dodged Erna Sue. She ate lunch with the French students and pretended to have fun. Boris ate lunch with Erna Sue. Arabelle sat so she could watch them. They didn't seem to miss her. They didn't look at her once as far as she could tell. From time to time they laughed over something Boris said. Arabelle wondered what was so funny. They were probably laughing about her. It was the longest week of her life.

On Friday, Boris waylaid her in the lunch line. "You act silly. Erna Sue act silly. Time you stop." She let him drag her to their table.

"Okay if I join you?" Arabelle asked.

Erna Sue glanced up from her fruit salad. "Sure."

"I don't want to intrude." Two high roads in one week would guarantee her sainthood.

"You're not." Erna Sue smiled, her eyes lowered.

After four days of not speaking, Arabelle didn't know

where to begin. She and Erna Sue traded wary looks.

"You're still mad, aren't you?" Erna Sue said.

"No, I'm not. I never was — or not for long."

"I don't know what I did, Alex."

Arabelle hesitated. This was going to be harder than she thought. "You said that Mrs. Cushman didn't blink on purpose and that she didn't almost smile."

"Based on scientific fact, Alex. When you have advanced Alzheimer's —"

"Why are you so sure of everything? You make the rest of us feel like dummies. Can't you let someone else be right once in a while?"

Erna Sue shrugged, a habit she had picked up from Boris. "If you want." She scooped up the last of her cottage cheese. "I'm not pretty or popular, Alex, and I'm no one's Mount Everest. What I am is smart, so why should I hide the fact?"

"You pretty," Boris said, faking a swoon.

Erna Sue blushed. "Look again. What you see is straight brown hair and glasses and a nose that's too big for my face."

"Your nose is fine," Arabelle said, at a loss for what else to say. She and Erna Sue stood on opposite shores, separated by miles of water. But at least they were speaking. She'd have to be satisfied with that for now.

That afternoon the cast rehearsed the end of act two when the Sycamore's cellar blows up. Mr. Zee instructed Arabelle ahead of time about the sound equipment.

"Controls are sensitive, Arabelle. The volume needle's jittery. Keep your eye on it." Mr. Zee set the volume to where he wanted it. "You okay with this?"

"Totally. I'm good with machines." She hoped that would be the case. The equipment seemed to have a mind of its own, the way it hummed and glowed.

This was the first rehearsal with sound effects. Mr. Zee had put her in charge of the doorbell and the phone, along with explosions and prompting.

The actors started the scene at the point where three G-men burst in to arrest Ed Carmichael for printing "Dynamite the Government" fliers and discover a stockpile of fireworks in the cellar.

Arabelle stood by the soundboard, her finger poised, and listened closely for a G-man to accuse Ed of inciting revolution, and for the other G-men to discover the 4th of July explosives. She checked the volume needle. Was it her imagination or had it moved? She couldn't remember exactly where Mr. Zee had set it and there wasn't time to find out. Grandpa delivered the cue line. Closing her eyes, Arabelle twisted the dial:

BOOM!

The blast rocked the auditorium and brought Mr. Villiers, the principal, on the run. "What's going on?" he shouted, charging through the door.

Arabelle rushed wild-eyed from the wings. "The needle jumped. It won't happen again." No one heard her over the pandemonium. Most of the cast had collapsed with heart failure. Mr. Zee tackled Mr. Villiers in the aisle.

"It's not a bomb, it's a recording," he yelled.

Arabelle crept to the edge of the stage. "I'm sorry, Mr. Villiers. Mr. Zee, I'm sorry," which didn't begin to describe her anguish.

Mr. Villiers's secretary stuck her head in the door. "Shall I call the police?"

"No need," Mr. Villiers said. "Everything's under control. Do me a favor, Walt. Put someone else on your soundboard."

Arabelle couldn't hear what Mr. Zee said back, but in her heart she knew she was toast. After this last screw-up, he would never give her another chance.

Chip showed her how to control the volume gauge. "Don't let the needle wander beyond this point."

This time the thundering explosion was exactly right, and the scene went off without a hitch: Mrs. Kirby and Alice screamed on cue. Tony knocked a chair over rushing to their side. Penelope dove for her copy of *Sex Takes A Holiday* while Ed rushed to save his xylophone. Kolenkhov, waving his arms wildly, dashed this way and that, bumping into Essie and the furniture. Only Grandpa, seated at the dining room table, his chin in his hand, took the mayhem in stride. "'Well, well, well,'" he said, smiling to himself while the uproar went on around him.

Mr. Zee jumped to his feet. "Well done!" he cried, which was a pretty good note to end Friday on.

Before she left, Arabelle apologized to the cast for her latest failure. To her astonishment, Bonnie said,

"Accidents happen, Alex. No one's perfect." Arabelle took her at her word.

Erna Sue waited in the lobby. "Mr. Zee plans to call Trish, Alex. I thought I should tell you."

"How do you know?"

"He asked if I had her phone number."

"He's going to replace me, isn't he?" She prayed Erna Sue would say no.

"Looks like it. I'm sorry." Erna Sue hesitated. "Maybe Trish won't be available."

"He'll find someone else."

"Wait and see." Erna Sue set off down the hall.

"Aren't you going home?" Arabelle called. She wanted company, someone to sound off to, a friend who would sympathize and make her feel better.

"Debate Club is holding a practice session. We debate DeWitt High next week. They're better than us."

Not for long, Arabelle thought. Not with you on the team.

The late bus waited out front, its motor idling. Arabelle climbed in and made straight for the back seats where the losers sat.

Why couldn't she do anything right? No matter how hard she tried, she screwed up. And now as a reward, Mr. Zee would replace her with Trish. She couldn't stand by and let that happen — not without a last-ditch effort to change his mind. But how? Mr. Villiers had said she should go and his word was law.

"Your stop," the bus driver yelled.

She trudged up the aisle and waited on the top step. "My life totally sucks," she said.

"Yeah? Mine's not so hot, either." The driver gave her a gruff smile and plenty of time to clear the doors before he closed them.

She did not share the day's terrible events with her parents, who were out for the evening. She ate standing at the fridge, undecided about her next step, and somehow managed to finish her homework. Was it too late to call him? What if he was in bed and the phone woke him? She'd be more than toast. She'd be yesterday's lunch.

She looked up his number and with a shaky finger dialed. One ring, two rings, three rings. Perhaps he was a sound sleeper. Perhaps he was out.

"This is Walt Zacharias. Sorry I missed your call. Leave your number and a short message and I'll get back to you." Beep.

Her words tumbled out. "Mr. Zee, it's me. I feel so bad about this afternoon I know you want to replace me I don't blame you it's just that — please, please don't get someone else — give me one more chance I know I can be the best prompter —" Beep, Beep.

Arabelle fell back across her bed, the phone clamped to her ear. She had squeezed the most important part of her message between beeps. Her fate was in his hands.

Mrs. Cushman

"But you promised," Arabelle said. "I was counting on you." This was the morning she and Boris planned to scale Mrs. Cushman's wall of silence. Instead, Boris and Chip were painting scenery.

"I know, I know. Mr. Zee say stage set come before home for babushka. Maybe I take sick and no paint."

"You can't do that. Why isn't the stage crew painting?"

Boris shrugged. "Big soccer game with St. Joe's."

"Never mind. I'll go to Heavenly Rest by myself." Another setback to contend with. Worse yet, she still didn't know if Mr. Zee had replaced her. She'd have to wait until Monday to find out.

Mr. Huckabee sat by the front door when she pedaled up the drive. He hunched forward in his wheelchair. "Cat got your tongue, Clarabelle?"

"My name's Arabelle," she said loudly.

"What're you so grumpy about?"

"I'm not grumpy. You are!"

"Well, I wouldn't be if you gave me a smile now and then."

"You said smiling is a waste of time."

"From most folks it is. Not from you."

Arabelle was not immune to a compliment, even from a grouch. She smiled at Mr. Huckabee. Mr. Huckabee smiled back.

Happy hailed her outside the rec room. "I have a favor to ask, Arabelle. Will you sit awhile with Mrs. Cushman so Lana can take a break? We're keeping Mrs. Cushman in bed today."

"Is she sick?"

"She has a touch of bronchitis. Bed is the best place for her. But we need someone to keep an eye on her."

"I don't mind." Anything was better than the rec room.

"Oh, good!" Lana said, when Arabelle appeared in the doorway. "I got a heap of work waiting. You be okay here?"

"Fine, Lana. What do you want me to do?"

"Nothing to do, honey. Just sit. Miz Cushman ain't going nowhere."

Mrs. Cushman, bolstered by pillows, was propped up in bed, a yellow ribbon tied around her hair that matched her yellow bed jacket. She gave no sign that anyone was in the room.

"Hi, Mrs. Cushman." Arabelle touched her lightly on

the shoulder. Nothing. Absolutely nothing. Whatever she was staring at had her in its grip.

Arabelle sat in the old-fashioned rocker beside the bed and stared out the window. After an eternity of staring on both their parts, she checked the time. Five minutes had passed.

Most of the rooms at Heavenly Rest reminded Arabelle of a hospital, but not Mrs. Cushman's. A chest of drawers painted apple green stood against the far wall. The chest looked very old and had a lace doily on top.

Arabelle wandered around, a visitor to Mrs. Cushman's past. She studied several framed photographs of a young man in a sailor uniform, his cap tipped at a jaunty angle. A faint signature on one said "To Peggy, with all my love, Pete." Other photographs of smiling adults and children in party dresses caught her attention. One photo of Mrs. Cushman at the piano looked just like her, only much, much younger.

A partly opened dresser drawer drew her eye. On closer inspection, she discovered a scrapbook covered in satin and tied with ribbon. Mrs. Cushman surely wouldn't mind if she took a peek inside. She carried the scrapbook to the rocker and sat with it on her knees. She had nothing to hide. Mrs. Cushman still stared into space.

As Arabelle turned the pages, letters and dried flowers spilled from the album. She gathered them up and tucked the flowers back between the leaves. She had no intention of reading the many love letters. That would be going too far. One of the letters that she didn't read was from Pete.

It started "Dearest, darling Peg."

There were a million letters from Pete and more photos of him in his uniform. The letters left no doubt that Pete and Peg were madly in love and planned to marry after his return from the South Pacific. Arabelle so hoped this had happened and that the wedding ring on Mrs. Cushman's finger was the one Pete gave her. She turned another page. More pictures, and — she caught her breath — a wedding photo of Pete and Peg smiling radiantly at the camera. The date on the wedding invitation was June 1946. Mrs. Cushman was twenty years old. Several pages later Arabelle came across a song in Pete's handwriting, entitled, "Peg O' My Heart." Sight-reading the notes, she sang the words quietly. The melody was pretty, the words old-fashioned:

"'Peg O' My Heart, I love you,
We'll never part, I love you,
Dear little girl, sweet little girl,
Sweeter than the rose of Erin,
Are your winning smiles endearin',
Peg O' My Heart, your glances
Make my heart say, "How's chances?"
Come be my own, come make your home in my heart.'"

How romantic! She tried to imagine the man of her dreams writing a song just for her. She sang the verse again, a bit louder this time, and looked up. Mrs. Cushman's eyes were dark empty rooms.

Arabelle bent closer and peered into her face. "Shall I sing 'Peg O' My Heart' again?" Maybe Mrs. Cushman only responded to gypsy songs. "I'll sing it again," she said, and because Pete must have held her hand when he sang to her, she took the limp hand in hers and sang the verse once more, her eyes fixed on Mrs. Cushman's face. Arabelle squeezed the frail fingers gently.

"Please squeeze back. I know you can," she prompted in a whisper. Wait — there! A slight twitch of the fingers, she was sure of it, would swear to it. Perhaps she could coax another twitch or two from those fingers.

But at that moment Lana breezed into the room.

"Guess what happened, Lana?"

"You better tell me, honey, or I'll be guessing all night."

"Mrs. Cushman squeezed my hand."

"You sure? Miz Cushman hasn't squeezed in a long time."

"Pretty sure." Arabelle stroked Mrs. Cushman's cheek. How cool it felt. If only they had had a little longer. They were so close.

Lana's eye fell on the open scrapbook and sheet of music. "When she first came here, Miz Chapman had that old scrapbook out a hundred times a day."

"How many years has she been here, Lana?"

"'Bout seven, eight years. Back then she was sharper, not like now."

"And Mr. Cushman?" The love of Mrs. Cushman's life must be very old.

"He passed last year."

"Oh, no —"

"That's right, honey. Took us by surprise. We were all expecting Miz Cushman to pass first."

"Does she know?"

"Can't tell what she knows and what she don't know. Before he passed, he came every day to see her. They were a pair."

Arabelle found Happy working at the nurse's desk. "You'll never guess what happened."

"Something wonderful, by the look on your face," Happy said.

"I sang 'Peg O' My Heart' to Mrs. Cushman. She squeezed my fingers."

"Aren't you the clever one. None of us thought to do that."

"Maybe she thought I was Pete — Mr. Cushman. I wouldn't mind if she did."

Happy patted Arabelle's hand. "She may have. Peter Cushman was a loving and devoted husband to the very end."

"Next week I'll break through, you'll see. I'll hold a picture of Pete in front of her nose and I'll sing 'Peg O' My Heart' and she'll smile." She hoped Happy would agree.

"We can do many things if we've a mind to, Arabelle, but not all things. Mrs. Cushman is no longer able to smile, but if she could, you'd be the one to make it happen, that much I do know."

"I can't wait 'til next week. I'm going back tomorrow."

Arabelle had just told her parents about Mrs. Cushman squeezing her fingers. "Lana says Mrs. Cushman hasn't squeezed for ages. Happy says that if Mrs. Cushman could smile, I'd be the one to make her. I mean to try." She checked the two bent heads across the kitchen table. Her father grunted, his standard reply when he was correcting exams. "Don't get your hopes up. In the final stages of Alzheimer's, the ability to respond is severely limited."

"Daddy, you weren't there."

Her usually optimistic mother looked up from her crossword. "Your father's right, I'm afraid."

"Well maybe you're both wrong."

Her mother went back to her crossword.

"Mr. Cushman wrote the neatest song for Mrs. Cushman. He called it 'Peg O' My Heart.'" Her parents exchanged a smile. "What? Have I said something funny?"

"'Peg O' My Heart' is an old, old song," Mrs. Archer said. "It's been around a long time."

"You mean Mr. Cushman didn't write it?" They could be wrong about this, too.

"No, sweetie. But that doesn't mean the song isn't very special to Mrs. Cushman. The specialness is what's important."

Mr. Archer scrawled a C- on a test booklet. "Sing us the song, Belle. It's been years since I heard it."

She cleared her throat and began. "'Peg O' My Heart, I love you, we'll never part, I love you . . .'"

"Very nice," her father said when she had finished. "Some of the best songs are from the past."

"'You must remember this, a kiss is still a kiss . . .'" her mom crooned with a goofy smile. "We danced to it. Remember, Lyman?"

"You bet." He looked at her with a glint in his eye and she flirted back like she was sixteen and on her first date.

Arabelle beat a fast retreat. At their ages, her parents should be past all that.

She biked out to Heavenly Rest the following afternoon. Mr. Huckabee was not outside waiting, and she had a smile all prepared. Then she remembered it was naptime. Naps were important at Heavenly Rest — almost as important as meals.

She let herself in and sped undetected down the Aloha corridor. Mrs. Cushman's room was empty. Her wheelchair stood in its accustomed place, but the framed photographs on the dresser and tables were missing. The bed had been stripped of sheets, the coverlet folded neatly at the foot. Mrs. Cushman couldn't have strayed far — not in her condition. The dresser drawers were empty when she looked. Happy must have moved her to another room.

Lana sailed into the room and stopped short, her hand clamped to her mouth. "Oh! We didn't expect you."

"Where's Mrs. Cushman, Lana?"

"I'll get Miss Happy. Don't go away."

Arabelle sat on the edge of the bed and waited. Before long Happy came in and sat beside her, Mrs. Cushman's scrapbook under her arm.

"What's happened? Where's Mrs. Cushman?"

"She went home last night," Happy said in a soft voice.

"How could you let her? She was in no shape to go home —"

"Arabelle, Mrs. Cushman passed on."

"She died? But she couldn't have! She squeezed my hand, Happy. How could she die?"

"Maybe she was ready to go, Arabelle. Maybe you were there to smooth the way, to sing one last song to her."

Arabelle didn't know what to say. She held fast to Happy's hand, her throat tight.

"How did she — You know —"

"Peacefully. Her heart simply gave out."

"I'd like to look at her scrapbook once more," Arabelle said, after they had sat for the longest time in silence. She turned the pages slowly, lingering longest over Pete's song to the girl of his dreams.

"I hope Peggy and Pete are together," she said in a shaky voice. "Do you think they are?"

"I'm sure of it."

She consoled herself with the thought of the Cushmans laughing and holding hands. Mrs. Cushman was young and pretty and Mr. Cushman young and handsome, and they were in love. What was the point of dying if you couldn't go back to an earlier, happier time?

Happy agreed.

When she told her parents what had happened, her mother said, "How lucky that you found Mrs. Cushman's scrapbook."

"The scrapbook didn't matter, Mom. It didn't keep her alive. She was ready to die."

"Maybe Happy's right," her father said, considering the possibility. "Maybe you smoothed the way."

"If only she had smiled — just once. Now she won't ever."

Later on the phone, Erna Sue said, "I'm sorry, Alex, but I did warn you."

"Thanks a lot, Erna Sue. That is so helpful!"

When Boris heard, he said "Mrs. Cushman smile for sure. Maybe not with mouth, but with heart, which is better than mouth because heart no lie."

Arabelle's eyes filled with tears. His words were the ones she most needed to hear.

The Rehearsal from Hell

Jeff Anderson was waiting for her Monday morning.

"You're late, Shorty."

"No kidding!" Arabelle, in low spirits after losing Mrs. Cushman, was not ready to joke with Jeff Anderson. She shoved her gym bag and coat into her locker and tried to close the door.

Jeff eyed the jumble. "You got too much stuff in there."

"Look who's talking!"

"Yeah, but my locker's neat." He shouldered her aside and eased the door shut.

"What would I do without you?" she scoffed.

"Dunno. It'd be tough." He fell into step beside her. "So how come you're called Alex?"

"Jeff, why aren't you in homeroom?" She didn't want to talk about Deirdre. She didn't want to talk — period.

"Cause I'm curious. Is Alex your middle name?"

"Not really. It's a joke. You wouldn't be interested."

"Guess again, Shorty. Tell me why and I'll tell you my middle name."

"What kind of trade is that?" Did he think she was stupid as well as short?

"Wait'll you hear what it is."

"What is it?"

"Uh-uh, you first."

"You'll make fun of me."

"No, I won't. I promise."

She almost believed him. "Alex is short for Alexis. Alexis is Deirdre Glendenning's middle name, a name I wish I had. Now you know."

"Whoa!" Jeff laughed. "Where'd you find a name like that?"

"In a novel."

"What's the novel? I might want to read it." They stood outside her homeroom.

"Ravished!"

"Sounds hot." He lifted an eyebrow. She bet he practiced that in the mirror, too.

"The hot parts aren't described."

"Bummer! Those are the best parts."

Her sentiments, exactly. "Your turn, Jeff." By now she was curious. Homeroom could wait.

"What?"

"Don't pretend. You know what."

Jeff studied her feet. He wasn't going to tell her.

"I'm waiting." She tapped her foot.

He looked up with a grin. "Egmond. Jeffrey Egmond Anderson the Third."

"You're kidding."

"Nope." They stared at each other and burst out laughing. After yesterday, she had doubted that she'd ever laugh again.

His name followed her from class to class like a knight on horseback. She scribbled Egmond in the margins of her notebook, delighted by the novelty and the pleasing sound of Egmond when she spoke it aloud.

Arabelle was five minutes late to rehearsal. In her rush down the aisle, she collided with Mr. Zee.

"Easy, Arabelle." He put out a hand to steady them both.

"Am I replaced? Did you get my call? I should've left my number. The beeps were awfully close together —"

"Arabelle," Mr. Zee lowered his voice, "I haven't replaced you, but you've got to calm down. You're making the actors nervous. You're making me nervous."

"I just want to be the best prom —"

"Let's settle for steady, okay? There's a naval expression, 'steady as she goes.' That's what I want you to be — steady as a ship in wind and currents."

"I can do that!" He was giving her another chance. She vowed to try harder. She would be the Queen Mary — steady, reliable, unsinkable.

Act three began on the wrong note. "Hold it!" Mr. Zee

called from three rows back. The actors on stage stopped. "You're much too cheerful. You've just spent the night in jail. Remember? Mrs. Kirby has been strip-searched. Mr. Kirby's arrest is the scandal of Wall Street. Alice has broken up with Tony. The Kirbys want nothing more to do with Alice's family or Alice. This is not cause for celebration. Let's try the scene again."

Arabelle had her hands full with sound effects and prompting. Her first and most important task of the afternoon was to label the dials on the soundboard so she wouldn't ring the doorbell instead of the phone or blow up the cellar by mistake. Bonnie still ad-libbed, which drove everyone crazy — Arabelle the most.

Mr. Zee constantly interrupted. "Bonnie, I want you to memorize your part, word for word. No more ad-libbing, am I clear?"

A moment later, he broke in again. "Grandpa, you're blowing the most important line in the play. When Mr. Kirby says, 'A man can't give up his job,' and you say 'Why not? You got all the money you need,' what do you say next?"

"I don't remember."

"Arabelle, what does Grandpa say next?"

"'You can't take it with you!'"

"Now why do you suppose that line is important?" Mr. Zee asked.

"It's the name of the play," Grandpa said sheepishly.

Mr. Zee nodded. "That's one reason. What's the other reason? Anyone?"

"Money isn't everything," Chip said. "Be happy and don't spend your life doing things you don't want to for the sake of money,"

"Because," Mr. Zee called, "you can't take it with you!"

Rehearsal ended later than usual. Crossing the lobby, Arabelle ran smack into Jeff Anderson.

"Thought I'd missed you, Shorty."

She backed away in surprise. "What're you doing here?"

"Waiting for you. Hey, you won't blab my middle name to anyone, will you?"

"Who would I tell?"

"Your friend Irma Sue."

"Erna, not Irma. She couldn't care less what your middle name is, Jeff. Erna Sue isn't into names. Besides, Egmond isn't so bad. I kind of like it."

"You do? God, I think it's terrible."

"That's because it's yours." Flustered, she threw on her coat and ran for the door.

"Hey, where you going?"

"Home. I take the late bus."

If she stayed a moment longer, Jeff would expect her to be funny and the bus would leave without her.

She sat by herself, halfway back. It had occurred to her in Health Science that Egmond was the perfect name for a hero in an adventure romance novel. Perfect, in fact, for *Ravished!* She made up a new chapter on the ride home:

. . . *The Earl of Egmond, né Denys Fitzroy, reared up in the stirrups, sword drawn, and drove his foaming steed toward the limp body that swung from an oak. With a mighty slash, Egmond's sword cut the rope. Jumping from the saddle, Denys Fitzroy gathered the girl in his arms and stroked her tender cheeks and flowing hair. Her eyelids fluttered . . .*

"What's your name, fair maiden?"

"Deirdre, sire, Deirdre Glendenning."

"Sacre bleu! Not the great actress —"

"Yes, sire, I am she."

"But what doth you in a tree, Deirdre?"

"Bandits, sire, intent on mischief, waylaid me on my morning ride. They stole my horse and left me to die."

"I will scour the kingdom, Deirdre, I will run them to ground . . ."

"Your stop!" the driver yelled. "Any better?" he asked as she passed.

"Yes, thanks."

"Likewise."

They smiled at each other.

The cast spent the next several days grinding through the third act.

On Thursday the Grand Duchess Olga Katrina, an old friend of Kolenkhov's from Czarist Russia, appeared for the first time, trumpeting her lines in a thick Russian accent as she swept around the stage. The actors collapsed in stitches.

"That's enough!" Mr. Zee thundered. "Let's wind up. In the play's final scene Grandpa convinces Mr. Kirby to quit the job he hates for a life of simple pleasures. Tony and Alice kiss and make up. The curtain falls as the Grand Duchess, who hasn't had a decent meal since leaving Russia, serves everyone blintzes that she's whipped up in the Sycamore kitchen."

"She doesn't serve the blintzes in the playbook, Mr. Zee," the Grand Duchess said.

"I know she doesn't, but that's what I want you to do. Director's prerogative."

Mr. Zee made them repeat the scene until he was satisfied. "First run-through tomorrow. We won't stop for mistakes. Bonnie, I expect you to know your lines cold. We have two weeks left to pull this off."

The following day, rehearsal clipped along at a steady pace. The phone and doorbell rang when they were supposed to and the cellar blew up on cue. Kyra danced like an ostrich, and in their big love scene, Chip kissed Bonnie as though he meant it and Bonnie controlled herself and didn't rip his shirt off.

At the end of act one, Mr. Zee called a brief time out.

Arabelle flew to the lobby and took the stairs two at a time. The juice machine outside the cafeteria ate three quarters and a dollar bill before she realized it was out of order. The bottled water machine would have to do. When she returned to the auditorium, the second act had begun. At first she noticed nothing amiss. Then she did.

Her dial labels were missing. They had to have fallen off. She groped around on the floor and found a wad of gum and a candy wrapper, but no labels. Someone had stolen them. She was the victim of sabotage. Her eye lit on Bonnie Atwood, three feet away, waiting to make an entrance.

"Have you seen my labels?" she asked. She wouldn't accuse Bonnie outright. Even serial killers deserved the benefit of the doubt until proven guilty.

"What labels, Alex? I've no idea what you're talking about." Her apple-cider smile didn't fool Arabelle for a minute.

Bonnie pranced out on stage humming a little tune. Arabelle grabbed her playbook and followed along.

Bonnie had ten short speeches before she exited through the door to the kitchen. She recited only one correctly. The confusion on stage grew as Bonnie ad-libbed wildly, which made the actors mix up their lines. To make matters worse, the doorbell was supposed to ring in exactly five seconds.

Arabelle's fingers hovered over the dials. This one must be the doorbell, had to be. She turned the dial. The phone rang! Don't panic, Arabelle. Stay calm. Okay, this is the dial. Please, please let this be the dial.

BOOM!

"Arabelle, come out here!" Mr. Zee shouted.

She rushed from the wings, close to tears. "Someone took my labels."

"Who took Arabelle's labels?" Mr. Zee asked.

No one, apparently.

"I'll help you re-label," Chip told her. "You're doing fine." But they both knew she wasn't.

The act continued.

"'Pirouette! Pirouette!'" Boris called, as Kolenkhov and Essie started their big dance scene. "'A little freer with the hands. The whole body must work!'" While Ed banged away on the xylophone, Kolenkhov spun wildly on one foot, showing Essie the way he wanted her to pirouette.

Her arms slicing air, Kyra leapt and twirled faster and faster around the dining room table. So fast, in fact, that when she tried to stop, she couldn't — not all at once, not until she crashed into the snake tank, knocking it off the sideboard. The tank landed on its side.

In an instant garter snakes slithered and writhed in every direction. Bonnie, screeching in panic, scrambled onto the dining room table. Kyra, who hated snakes as much as Bonnie, tried to climb aboard but Penelope and Grandpa got there ahead of her. Bonnie was still shrieking when a snake slithered over Kyra's foot. Screaming for dear life, Kyra dove off the stage feet-first and landed with a whump.

Mr. Zee raced down the aisle.

The cast gathered around Kyra, who rocked in pain over her ankle. Mr. Zee yelled, "Get the nurse, Erna Sue. Kyra's hurt herself."

"You think it's broken?" She turned a teary face to Mr. Zee, who looked mighty worried.

He patted her hand. "Easy, Kyra. We'll have you fixed up in no time."

"We'll need an X-ray," the school nurse said after she had examined Kyra's ankle. "Let's get an ice pack on this.

Can you walk?"

Arabelle and Erna Sue helped Kyra take a few hopping steps. "I can't," she whimpered.

"Allow me," Chip said. He picked Kyra up in his arms and carried her out of the auditorium to the nurse's office. Chip to the rescue, Arabelle thought. He always knows what to do.

Boris and Mr. Zee quickly rounded up snakes and dropped them in the tank. One snake was missing. Bonnie refused to budge from the table until it was caught.

"This rehearsal is over," Mr. Zee announced in a grim voice. "Go on home, all of you."

"We've got to catch that snake," Arabelle said. She and Boris stood apart from the others. Erna Sue joined them. Boris shrugged. "Snake no come back."

"It will when it's hungry," Erna Sue said. "Pet snakes don't hunt for themselves."

"Maybe we feed," Boris joshed. "What they eat?"

"What *do* they eat. Baby mice and earthworms, sometimes fish."

Boris grinned and put his arm around her. "You so smart. How you know that?"

Erna Sue blushed. She didn't appear to mind his arm in the least. "The Learning Channel devoted two shows to ophidiology. That's the study of snakes."

Arabelle looked from one to the other. "What are we going to do?" she asked, reminding them of her presence.

Before they could devise a plan, Lizbeth Keppel struck a blow for big behinds. Leaping from the wings, she danced around the dining room table, jabbing the missing snake at Bonnie. "Take this! And this! And this!"

Bonnie's mouth flew open. Out burst a fresh torrent of shrieks.

Mr. Zee shouted, "That's enough, Lizbeth! Bonnie, get down!"

Bonnie, wild-eyed and pale, leapt off the table and fled through the emergency exit backstage. With a pleased smile, Lizbeth dropped the last snake into the tank.

On their way out, Arabelle said to Erna Sue and Boris, "What if Kyra's sprained her ankle?"

"She probably twisted it, Alex. You can twist an ankle without spraining it."

"Play no happen if Kyra sprain herself."

Erna Sue replied briskly, "Gymnasts perform with sprained ankles all the time."

"But what if it's broken?" Arabelle asked.

For once Erna Sue had no answer. They stood together in the lobby, each waiting for the other to offer a solution, should the worst come to pass.

"Maybe I could play Essie," Arabelle said, "— only if Kyra can't, of course." Never in a million years would she wish Kyra in a cast or on crutches. Still, faced with such a calamity, wasn't she the perfect choice to star in the play and be the funniest Essie Carmichael that ever lived?

"Da!" Boris clapped her on the shoulder.

Arabelle glowed. One down, one to go.

"Mr. Zee doesn't use understudies, Alex, remember?"

"I'm not an understudy. I'm a prompter."

"You don't toe dance," Erna Sue reminded her. "Essie's a toe dancer."

"You keep telling me that. I could learn. I know I could."

"In two weeks? I don't think so."

Arabelle faked a smile. She wished she had kept her mouth shut. She wished that Erna Sue didn't always find reasons to doubt her. Good friends should believe in one another and offer encouragement.

"I guess we'll never know who's right," Arabelle grumbled. She had no doubt about who was right, only that she would never have the chance to prove herself, unless, by some miracle, the unthinkable happened.

To the Rescue

When Arabelle told her parents what had happened, her mother said, "A bad rehearsal is good luck, sweetie. It means opening night will be a success." No one put the best face on catastrophe like her mother.

"Rubbish! Pure superstition," her father replied. "A bad rehearsal is a bad rehearsal — nothing more."

Arabelle wasn't so sure. "According to Mr. Zee, you wish an actor good luck by saying 'break a leg.' Otherwise the actor has an accident. Like poor Kyra."

Her father grunted. "Kyra hurt herself because of ophidiophobia — fear of snakes. Telling her to break a leg would not have helped. What helps is overcoming your fear of snakes."

Her mother chimed in, "But if someone had told her to break a leg, maybe she'd have danced less energetically and not crashed into the snake tank."

Another grunt. "Telling someone to break a leg is as ridiculous as not using the elevator on Friday the 13th."

"I certainly don't, Lyman."

"I do, Marian. So far I've survived unscathed."

Arabelle didn't stick around for the rest of the argument. Like Erna Sue, her father rarely lost.

The next morning, she grabbed her bike and headed out to Heavenly Rest. She had been too late to help Mrs. Cushman, but Mr. Wexler was a different story. Surely the happy ending that a new word would signal couldn't be far off. She pedaled faster, anticipating his breakthrough moment. Smiling, she wondered how Mrs. Becker would entertain them during juice and cracker break and whether she and Mr. Huckabee would trade insults, which all by itself was entertaining. Maybe this morning Mr. Rosen would remember to put his clothes on. She had never seen him with his clothes on. A mile down the road her cell phone rang. She pulled over and stopped.

"Arabelle?"

"Is that you, Mr. Zee?" She'd know his voice anywhere.

"Good. I caught you. We need to talk."

Arabelle straddled her bike. "Have I done something wrong?"

"Not yet. Kyra just called. Her ankle's broken."

"Oh, no!"

"She's in a cast. I have to replace her." Arabelle waited through a charged silence. "How much of the play do you know by heart?

"Most of it." For once she didn't exaggerate.

"How about Essie's lines?"

"Well, sure. After four weeks of prompting —"

"Good! Good! I'd like you to play Essie."

She held tight to her cell phone while she tried to make sense of his words. He couldn't possibly have said what she imagined. She must learn to listen more closely. Weren't her parents always on her about that? She would start Monday. No matter what was said to her, she would listen as though her life depended on every word.

"Arabelle, are you there? Did you hear me?"

She steadied her bike. "Are you asking me to play Essie?" she stammered. Maybe she had heard right.

"The part's made for you."

"Do you mean it?" Her bike fell over. He sounded quite serious.

"It'll take a lot of hard work. You game?"

She took a deep breath and exhaled slowly, which always helped when she hyperventilated. The victory dance would have to wait. "Oh gosh, yes! I'm totally game! But there are only two weeks left."

"Plenty of time. I wouldn't ask if I didn't think you could do it. Boris will help you. You'll need extra rehearsals since many of your scenes are together. I don't suppose you dance?"

"Sort of — a little —" She had seen *The Red Shoes* twice on cable and cried both times. "I don't have toe shoes."

"No toes. You can fake it. Balls of the feet are fine.

Flutter your arms but don't leap or twirl. When you do leg lifts, hold onto the furniture."

"I can do better than that," she cried. No way would she fake it. Despite heavy odds, her dearest wish had been granted. She'd learn ballet from the ground up and make Mr. Zee proud, and all the other doubters, starting with Erna Sue Comstock.

"But what about prompting? I'm not sure I can do both."

"You can't. I'll ask Trish."

"You wanted to replace me, didn't you? I'm sorry I wasn't better —"

"You're an actress, Arabelle, not a prompter. I spotted that when you tried out."

Never before had she received such a thrilling compliment. Mr. Zee was giving her the chance to be a great actress. He wouldn't be sorry, she'd see to that. Her screwing-up days were over.

. . . Alone on stage, Deirdre Glendenning sank to her knees, her hands clasped in prayer. "O Lord, deliver me from this villain!" Her voice trembled with passion as her green eyes swept the audience and lingered on the Earl of Egmond's rapt face. The opening night of Ravished!, *a new play by Sir Thomas Crookshank written specially for her, was about to take London by storm. Never again would the theatre be the same . . .*

Arabelle called Erna Sue right away. She couldn't scale the heights without the support of friends, nonbelievers included. When Erna Sue didn't answer, she tried again.

Still no answer. Disappointed, she hung up. She'd tell her friends at Heavenly Rest first. They were sure to cheer her on. She wouldn't have to prove herself to them.

Upon arriving, Arabelle dumped her bike in the bushes and ran straight to the rec room. Gwenda was leading the group in sing-along. Mouths already open stayed open in surprise when she charged through the door waving her arms dramatically.

"Guess what's happened? You'll never guess! Not in a million years —"

"Help me! Help me!" Mr. Wexler started from his chair.

"What's going on?" Mr. Rosen asked. "Is there a problem?" Arabelle hardly recognized him in trousers and a plaid jacket. He had forgotten to put on a shirt.

"Oh, my God!" Mrs. Becker gasped, her hand to her throat. "You can't be — tell us you're not!"

"Something the matter with Clarabelle?"

Mrs. Becker informed Mr. Huckabee under her breath.

"Speak up! I can't hear you."

"Well, you could if you'd put your hearing aids in," Mrs. Becker said.

Gwenda, smiling nervously, flipped through the songbook. "Why don't we all sing 'Wait 'Til The Sun Shines, Nellie' and let Arabelle catch her breath."

"Yes, you better sit down," Mrs. Becker advised. "You look quite peaked. It's no wonder in your condition."

"What are you talking about?" Arabelle asked, bewildered by their worried faces.

Mrs. Becker put a comforting hand on Arabelle's. "Are you planning to keep it, dahling?"

"Keep what, Mrs. Becker?"

"You know," she said with a sly look, "your little surprise package."

Arabelle had new respect for Boris. This is what it must be like if you didn't speak the same language as the people around you. "What surprise package, Mrs. Becker?"

"Your baby. It's all right if you don't want to tell us."

It took her a minute to run the gamut from disbelief to horror. "I'm not having a baby! I don't even have a boyfriend!"

Mr. Huckabee snorted. "Well, you would if you smiled more."

"Why don't we let Arabelle tell us what's happened," Gwenda suggested. "I'm sure she has exciting news for us."

"I do. I'm in the school play. I'm Essie Carmichael in *You Can't Take It With You,* and I toe dance." Why did this suddenly sound less exciting than having a baby?

Mrs. Becker clutched her heart. "How divine! I was in *You Can't Take It With You* and I stole the show."

"Who did you play?" Arabelle asked, curiosity overcoming her surprise package and what it implied.

"Guess!" Mrs. Becker dared her to get it right.

Arabelle wavered between boozy Gay Wellington and the Grand Duchess Olga Katrina. "Were you the Grand Duchess?"

"Of course, dahling. I was born to the role. Only great actresses play the Grand Duchess. I took seven curtain calls opening night."

"I'll be lucky to get one. I'm supposed to ballet dance, Mrs. Becker. I wish I knew how."

"Pish, there's nothing to it. Who wants to help teach Arabelle ballet?" Every hand in the room was raised.

Arabelle, touched by their offer, didn't know whether to laugh or cry. They believed in her and wanted to help. Even those in wheelchairs.

Mrs. Becker shoved her walker aside and struck a pose, knees bent outward, arms circled in front of her. "This is a plié," she said, and promptly lost her balance.

Gwenda caught her before she hit the floor. "We'd better stick to sing-along, Mrs. Becker."

"Piddle! We're going to teach Arabelle ballet. The Nellie song can wait. Come along, Mr. Rosen. You, too, Mr. Wexler. The rest of you stay put in your chairs."

Gwenda hovered in distress. "Mrs. Becker, please —"

"Stand aside, Gwenda." Mrs. Becker was every inch the Grand Duchess, to whom no one gave orders — certainly not Gwenda Watkins.

"Watch closely, child." Mrs. Becker tottered over to Mr. Rosen who held out his arms. "This is a glissade." Clutching one another for dear life, they glided in widening circles, slip-slide right, slip-slide left, slip-slide right. Mrs. Becker led. Arabelle giggled at the spectacle. She couldn't help herself.

Gwenda darted after them. "Please, Mrs. Becker. Mr. Rosen, please stop —"

"What in the world?" Happy Holliday stood in the

doorway. "A dance, as I live and breathe! What a merry scene! We must have music." She flew to the piano and banged out a tune.

Mr. Wexler made a beeline for Arabelle. "Help me! Help me!" he said, which she understood immediately. He was asking her to dance. She didn't need a boyfriend to figure that out. "I'd love to, Mr. Wexler." With his arm around her waist and her hand on his shoulder, he steered her across the floor.

It was slow going and a far cry from ballet, but she was having the best time. Her friends wanted her to succeed, Mr. Wexler wanted to dance with her, and hadn't he almost, but not quite, said, "May I have this dance?"

"Hold tight to Mr. Wexler, Arabelle," Happy cried. "Camille, you should be in your walker."

"A pox on it!"

"Mr. Rosen, hold tight to Mrs. Becker." Wheelchairs rolled up and down the room, in time to the tune that Happy played with joyful abandon. Arabelle and Mr. Wexler danced a two-step, keeping time to the music and "Help me!" Even Mr. Huckabee joined in. "Give us a push, Gwenda!" he cried, holding tight to the arms of his chair.

There was a burst of applause when the music stopped. Mrs. Becker fanned herself with a tissue. "I hope we've helped, dahling. Half the battle in ballet is executing a well-done glissade."

Somehow Arabelle managed a straight face. "Thanks, Mrs. Becker. You've helped a lot."

"Snack time," Gwenda said. This was greeted with more joy than usual. Happy helped Gwenda set out juice and crackers.

Mr. Wexler seemed lost in a happy memory. "Did you used to dance with Mrs. Wexler?" Arabelle asked him. He still had his hands around her waist. When he didn't answer, she asked again, "Did you, Mr. Wexler?"

He looked down at her and said softly, "Help me, help me."

"Can you say yes or no, Mr. Wexler?" She felt his hands tighten with the strain of trying. "When we danced, were you thinking of Mrs. Wexler? Just a tiny bit? Just for one sec?"

He tensed, his lips pursed. "Help me."

"That's okay, Mr. Wexler." She hid her disappointment behind a smile. He deserved her support, her belief in him, not a long face. "Sometimes things happen when you least expect it. Like me getting to play Essie Carmichael. One day soon, a new word will pop out of your mouth by accident. You'll see."

His eyes lit up, and with a gentle smile he let go of her.

Mrs. Becker thumped her walker on the floor for attention. "Let's help Arabelle with her lines. Come along, dahling, recite your lines. We'll be the audience."

This was hardly the audience Arabelle had in mind. "I'd rather not, Mrs. Becker. I didn't bring my playbook."

"A great actress does not procrastinate," Mrs. Becker chided. "How many weeks to opening night?"

"Two. Mr. Zee says there's plenty of time."

"Pooh! Two weeks is barely enough time."

"Help me! Help me!"

"Say your lines, dahling. Don't play hard to get."

"Say 'em loud enough so I can hear," Mr. Huckabee grumped.

They crowded around and gazed at her with unblinking attention.

For the life of her Arabelle couldn't remember one line. Why weren't Happy and Gwenda there to save her? She could hear their voices out in the hall.

As if on cue, Gwenda stuck her head in the door. "Happy and I will be right with you. Arabelle, take over."

"Looks like you're in charge, little lady," Mr. Rosen said.

Arabelle quickly checked her watch. "Isn't it almost time for lunch?"

"We have fifteen minutes, child."

"Help me! Help me!"

Mrs. Becker rapped for silence. "Act one, scene one," she said in her Grand Duchess voice. "The curtain rises. Penelope is at her typewriter. Essie enters from the kitchen, fanning herself. Line, Arabelle!"

Out tumbled the words. "'My, that kitchen's hot.'"

Mrs. Becker spoke the line along with her. "Fan yourself, dahling. Don't expect the audience to take your word for it. Next line!"

"'That candy I'm making won't get cool,'" Arabelle recited.

Mrs. Becker's voice rose and fell with her own. "No,

no, child. The line goes 'that new candy I'm making — it just won't ever get cool.'"

"Louder," Mr. Huckabee called.

"You're confusing me, Mrs. Becker." The shoe was on the other foot. She had done the same thing when she insisted actors be word perfect. She owed them an apology.

"Say the line again, dahling. See if you can get it right."

"Let her say it the way she wants," Mr. Rosen grumbled.

"Help me! Help me!"

Arabelle spoke her line at top speed, to throw Mrs. Becker off. Undaunted, Mrs. Becker recited the line a beat slower.

"I thought you were the Grand Duchess," Arabelle said, vexed and astonished by Mrs. Becker's memory of a part she had never played. "Why are you reciting with me?"

"I knew everyone's lines, child. I never forget lines. A great actress doesn't, you know."

Happy clapped her hands for attention. She and Gwenda had slipped back into the room moments earlier. "I've just had the best idea. Why don't we all go and see Arabelle opening night?"

"Hear hear!" Mr. Rosen said.

Arabelle stared in horror. "Oh, please don't. I'd be so nervous. I mean I'd love you to come, but — but — I'd bomb. Totally."

"Stuff and nonsense! We'll bring you good luck, dahling. Every great actress needs luck. Talent is not enough."

"Help me! Help me!"

She'd die if they came. Somehow she had to stop them, without hurting their feelings. Their feelings counted, but not on opening night, not if Mrs. Becker recited Essie's lines with her and Mr. Wexler cried out for help, not if Mr. Huckabee yelled at her to speak up or, worst of all, Mr. Rosen took his jacket off and he had nothing on underneath.

She looked in desperation at Happy. Happy mouthed back *don't worry*. But Arabelle did worry. She had to figure out how to keep them away. Their eager faces struck at her heart. A short time ago she had had such fun with them, but in a blink all that had changed. She felt awful, but she could not let them ruin her life. Her big chance might never come again.

Ten Easy Lessons

When Arabelle broke the news to her parents, her mother said, "That's terrific, sweetie. Is Essie the one who writes plays?"

"That's Penelope, Mom. Essie's the ballet dancer."

Her father puzzled over this latest turn of events. "Since when do you dance ballet?"

"I don't, Daddy. Not yet. But I will."

She had stopped by the town library on her way home and checked out *Ballet in Ten Easy Lessons*. The DVD featured Maria Tallchief, the famous ballerina, in *Swan Lake*.

Later that day Erna Sue called. "Have you heard? Kyra broke her ankle —"

"I know. Mr. Zee told me."

"He did?"

"Guess what? He wants me to play Essie." She could

imagine the look of shock on Erna Sue's face.

"He does? That's — that's wonderful."

Arabelle smiled to herself. "He says I'll be fine."

"You'll need a crash course in dancing, Alex."

"I don't have to dance on my toes, Erna Sue. Essie isn't a very good dancer, remember?"

"Yes, but you need to dance well enough to be bad. You'd better take lessons."

"I am." Arabelle ended the conversation before Erna Sue found out where the lessons were from.

After dinner she played the DVD from beginning to end. This was going to be harder than she thought. Ten easy lessons were anything but. She would concentrate her efforts on a few simple techniques that showcased her talent as a dancer as well as an actress.

Arabelle woke earlier than usual Sunday morning, pulled on tights and a pink tank top, and downed juice and a donut in the kitchen.

Her parents were in the family room drinking coffee and reading the paper.

"Would you mind sitting somewhere else?" she said.

"I guess we can," her father replied. "What's going on?"

"I need to learn ballet." She waved her DVD at him and switched on the TV.

"From a DVD?"

I only need the basic steps, Daddy. I've already mastered the glissade."

"We'll sit in the kitchen, sweetie." Her mother picked up the coffee cups and headed for the door. Shaking his head in disbelief, her father gathered up the stray sections of the paper.

"No peeking," Arabelle said. "I want to surprise you opening night."

She started the DVD and watched enthralled as Maria Tallchief in a white tutu of net and feathers danced her most famous role as a swan who falls in love with a prince and drowns after he two-times her. The ten lessons were at the end, with ballet steps in slo-mo.

Arabelle struck a ballet stance and with one hand held onto the back of a chair for balance.

"Jeté," the voice-over commanded. "Leap like a gazelle from one foot to the other."

She watched Maria do it, then leaped across the room and crashed into the fireplace tools, scattering shovel, poker, tongs, and broom.

"What happened?" her father yelled from the kitchen.

"Nothing, Daddy. Everything's cool."

"Arabesque," the voice commanded. "Raise your left leg behind you."

Maria's leg pointed skyward. Arabelle hoisted her leg as high as she could.

"Right arm forward, left arm up," the voice instructed.

The minute she let go of the chair she lost her balance. The brass floor lamp by the couch took the brunt and toppled over before she could catch it.

"What's happening?" her father called.

"The lamp was in the way," she yelled. "Don't worry, it didn't break." Her father never tired of asking the same question over and over. It must come from teaching.

"Attitude," the relentless voice continued. "Imitate a dying swan. Elevate your leg and bend your knee. Not too much!"

Really, who ever heard of a swan lifting its leg for any reason, let alone in its last moments of agony? She lifted her leg.

"Pirouette!"

"I can't," she said, glaring at the TV.

"Yes, you can," the voice intoned. "Rotate on one leg slowly, then faster as you gain confidence."

Arabelle twirled on one foot. She had no idea what to do with her other foot, but at least it wasn't on the floor. A second later she plowed into the pile of logs by the fireplace.

"Are you all right, sweetie?" Her mother hovered in the doorway.

"Mom! I don't want company. Go back to the kitchen." She sat in a heap of firewood while the DVD went on without her. "You can do this, Alex," she told herself. Didn't she top the charts when it came to stick-to-itiveness and resolve? Deirdre Glendenning would never settle for less than the best. And neither would she.

"Relevé," the voice commanded. Arabelle stopped the recording and started over at the beginning. Every sign pointed to a long, strenuous Sunday.

"Yo, Squirt, I hear you're in the school play," Jeff

Anderson said to her Monday morning.

"Who told you?" News traveled fast in high school, but this beat the record.

"Boris. I haven't read the play. Is it hot?"

What a question. "Massively, Jeff. It's got everything — nudity, orgies, sex fiends —"

Jeff grinned. "So who do you play?"

"I am Aphrodite, goddess of love. I turn hockey players into pucks."

Jeff started laughing. "Wait, I'll walk with you. Okay if I come to rehearsal, Shorty?"

"No! Rehearsals are closed. Mr. Zee is very strict about that."

"I won't say a word."

"Jeff, don't you understand no?"

"I like to keep my options open."

"You don't have options with Mr. Zee."

"How about with you?"

"I'm not in charge, Jeff. Mr. Zee is."

"Yeah, but what if you were?"

"It would depend."

"On what?"

"Lots of things."

"Such as?"

The bell rang before she could think of any.

At lunch, Arabelle planned her first rehearsal with Boris. Mr. Zee had rescheduled regular rehearsals so she and Boris could practice together ahead of time.

"Do you want me to sit in?" Erna Sue asked. "I don't mind."

"No thanks. I'll dance better if no one's watching." Erna Sue would point out every mistake and suggest ways to improve — nicely, of course, because Erna Sue didn't have a mean bone in her body.

"Alex, in two weeks the whole school will be watching."

"I know, but by then I won't be so terrible." She crossed her fingers under the table.

Boris went into his Kolenkhov act. "Soon you dance like angel, my little Essie." He lowered his voice. "Mr. Zee ask Trish Vogel to prompt."

Erna Sue raised her eyebrows. "And?"

"She say yes." They looked over at Bonnie's table where Trish always sat. Bonnie wasn't in her usual seat, nor anywhere in the cafeteria when they checked. Maybe she had stayed home with snakebite and rehearsal would be canceled. By 2:30 there still wasn't a notice on the board, which meant business as usual.

Arabelle hurried to the auditorium. Boris had turned on the stage lights. The rest of the hall lay in darkness. She put on her dance slippers while he tried out the xylophone.

"I'm ready," she said, which was far from the truth where ballet was concerned.

"We start from beginning," Boris said, flipping the playbook open.

"But our scene together is at the end of act one."

"Mr. Zee want from beginning. He want you say lines and dance."

"Oh, all right! Promise you won't laugh." They started with Essie's first entrance. Boris played all the parts except hers.

Arabelle jetéd and glissaded around the set, her arms whirring like windmills, and by some miracle completed the act without falling down.

There was a burst of applause when she had finished and collapsed in relief. Boris was not the one clapping. She jumped up and stared horrified into the darkness that almost, but not quite, hid Jeff Anderson. He sat halfway back, his feet propped on the seat in front of him like he owned the place.

"Jeff, this is a private rehearsal!"

"I won't say a word, Peanut. I'll be good."

"I can't do my best with you looking."

"I'm your inspiration. Every great artist has one."

She glared at him. "I refuse to go on!"

Jeff's feet hit the floor. "Ah, come on, Shorty, I'm harmless. Can I stay, Boris? Every great actress needs an audience."

Boris grinned at Jeff. "Da, okay, you stay."

The traitor Boris and God's gift to hockey were in cahoots. Very well. Since she was outnumbered, she'd make a total fool of herself in front of Jeff, after which she'd never speak to him again.

They started act one over. Her dancing was a little wilder this time. She wouldn't admit that she was trying to impress God's gift, who now sat in the front row.

After an arabesque with her leg a little too high and her arms a little too wild, she and the xylophone went down together.

Jeff sprang up on stage. "Yo, Shorty, you okay?"

She rocked back and forth, moaning, "I can't do Essie. I can't dance." Surely they'd say, yes, you can, you're the perfect Essie.

Neither of them said a word.

"I just need more practice." How could they not believe in her?

"Maybe better if arms and legs not so wild," Boris said.

"I got an idea, Peanut. Try this." Jeff dipped and swooped around the dining room table, his elbows stuck out at right angles; then, with a swivel, he skidded backwards to a stop. "What d'ya think?"

"You're making fun of me, Jeff Anderson. Essie's a dancer, not a hockey player."

"I'm trying to help, Shorty. How about it, Boris?"

"Da, she right."

Boris and Jeff studied Arabelle at length.

"Maybe move arms, but not legs," Boris suggested. "Like mermaid."

"What a wonderful idea!" Arabelle mocked. "Have you ever seen a dancer who didn't move her legs?"

"Get big laugh," Boris said with a grin. Jeff agreed. They celebrated with fist bumps.

Arabelle hated them both. "Essie is not a mermaid. I refuse to dance like one." They didn't take her seriously.

Here was her big chance to perform the role of her dreams, and they didn't care.

"I don't need your help. I'll do better on my own." She'd show them! For now she'd follow Mr. Zee's directions. In rehearsals she'd hold onto the furniture when she lifted her leg, but she'd practice in secret. By opening night she would achieve a halfway decent arabesque and leap like a gazelle, see if she wouldn't. Pirouettes, however, were out of the question.

"So what's the plan, Peanut?"

"Trying harder," she said, which was her solution to most problems. She kept this to herself for fear that Jeff and Boris would turn it into a hockey game or a Walt Disney special. She knew what she had to do, and no one — not Jeff, not Boris, not Erna Sue — would keep her from it.

One by one, the cast and crew straggled in. Jeff hung around until Mr. Zee appeared and shooed him out.

Arabelle handed Trish the playbook and showed her where to sit.

"How much prompting is there?" Trish asked.

"A fair amount. Bonnie forgets her lines a lot." Arabelle couldn't resist.

The cast watched in silence as Mr. Zee rolled his sleeves up, taking his time, left sleeve first, then the right, to one inch above the elbows. This had become a daily ritual that they were convinced kept bad luck away. None of them could explain why, since Kyra had broken her ankle on a rolled-up sleeve day.

"Where's Bonnie?" Mr. Zee asked, after counting

heads.

"No one's seen her."

"She wasn't in school today."

Mr. Zee's frown deepened. "Know where she is, Trish?"

"No, Mr. Zee. She isn't answering her cell."

"Okay. Erna Sue, read Alice's part until Bonnie shows up. Arabelle, I want you in a tutu tomorrow. You need to rehearse in costume."

"I don't have a tutu."

"I know you don't. Kyra's lending you one of hers. It's in the back. Try it on at home."

"A long tutu or a short tutu?" A short tutu would barely cover her hips. She might as well be naked!

"Short."

Boris and Chip laughed at her stricken face and Chip started again with the strippers' theme song.

"Let's go," Mr. Zee called. "Act one, from the beginning."

Penelope took her place at the typewriter. Arabelle had just made her entrance when the door in back of the auditorium opened and a short, round man barreled down the aisle and planted himself in front of the stage.

"Where's Walt Zacharias?"

"Right here." Mr. Zee strode down the aisle. "What can I do for you?"

"I'm Bonnie Atwood's father!"

"I'm afraid I don't —"

"My little girl spent the weekend in bed, Zacharias! In a darkened room! Do you know why?"

Mr. Zee narrowed his eyes.

"Nervous exhaustion, that's why! From emotional stress! Stress caused by snakes!"

"The snakes are harmless," Mr. Zee said, folding his arms.

"It's harassment, that's what it is. I've notified the animal rights people. They're mighty interested in you, as the principal of this school will be when I inform him about the snakes. Mrs. Atwood and I will not allow Bonnie to be in your play unless the snakes go and you apologize to our little girl for harassing her."

"Bonnie has not been harassed. The snakes are important to this play, Mr. Atwood. I guess we can use fake snakes if we have to —"

"No snakes! My little girl gets the heebie-jeebies at the thought of snakes. A fake snake will put her right back in bed."

"That's it, then. I'm sorry to lose Bonnie but I won't make concessions that undermine the play."

Mr. Atwood bounced in rage. "You telling me the snakes stay?"

"That's what I'm telling you. I'm prepared to use fake snakes if it'll help, but I'm damned if I'll write snakes out of the script."

"We'll see about that!" Mr. Atwood hurtled up the aisle and out the door.

Mr. Zee glowered at the retreating figure. The crew joined the cast on stage. No one knew what to say or how to help.

Chip cleared his throat. "Could Erna Sue play Alice —"

"No, thank you," Erna Sue said. "I'm not into acting, Chip. Besides, I think Alice is sappy."

"Why can't the snake tank be empty?" Arabelle asked. "The audience won't know the difference."

The PA system crackled to life. "Mr. Zee, please report to the principal's office immediately." Everyone recognized the dreaded voice of Mr. Villiers's secretary.

"We'll go with you, Mr. Zee," Chip said. "United we stand, divided we fall."

"No, Chip, this is my battle. The rest of you carry on. I'll join you when I can. Chip, you're in charge."

For Mr. Zee's sake, everyone tried extra hard. Arabelle danced the way Mr. Zee wanted her to, instead of the way she wanted to. Erna Sue read Alice's lines with spirit and didn't once sound disapproving. By the end of act one there was still no sign of Mr. Zee. Chip thought they should start act two. Penelope and Grandpa wanted to quit for the day. Boris said they should vote — after all, this was America.

A moment later the door to the auditorium opened, and Mr. Zee trudged down the aisle like he had a ten-ton sack of manure strapped to his back.

Arabelle knew without being told that the news was bad.

A Turn for the Worse

"Bad news, I'm afraid. I have to cancel the play."

Penelope burst into tears.

"You've been railroaded, Mr. Zee." Chip looked around angrily. "Who wants to go see Mr. Villiers with me?"

Arabelle jumped up. "I will. I do." She'd save the play single-handed if she had to.

"Hold on, Chip," Mr. Zee said. "The principal isn't the problem."

"Mr. Atwood wouldn't back down, is that it?"

"I'm afraid so. He vowed Bonnie would never return."

"I feel so responsible, Mr. Zee." Lizbeth verged on tears. "I wish I hadn't taunted her with that snake."

"What's done is done. No point crying over spilled milk."

"We need an understudy," Chip said, determined to

turn the tide.

Mr. Zee shook his head. "I never use them, Chip."

"What about Trish?" Arabelle cried. Trish Vogel was the perfect solution.

"We open in two weeks, Arabelle. She'd have too much to memorize."

"I could help her, Mr. Zee. I know most of Alice's lines." Arabelle willed him to say yes.

"Out of the question, I'm afraid."

For the second time that afternoon no one knew what to say or do.

"Go on home, everybody," Mr. Zee said. "It's getting late."

The cast and crew filed out of the auditorium in silence. Fighting back tears, Arabelle went to look at Kyra's tutu for her first and last time.

The pleated skirt, made of pink tulle and trimmed with rosebuds, surpassed her wildest dreams. She pictured herself pirouetting on stage to wild, sustained applause. Her deep curtsy brought the audience to its feet, shouting, "Encore! Encore!" Lost in the moment, she didn't hear Mr. Zee come up behind her.

"Arabelle, are you still here?"

She jumped a foot. "I wanted to look at Kyra's tutu, Mr. Zee." Her eyes filled with tears, which she didn't bother to hide.

Mr. Zee mustered a smile that, hard as she tried, she couldn't return. "I am sorry the play didn't work out, Arabelle. Maybe next year." He turned away abruptly.

Poor Mr. Zee. She had thought only of herself, not how he must feel. His disappointment must be as great as hers. Unsure what to say that would help, she debated whether to stay or leave. Sometimes you wanted company when you felt bad; other times you didn't. She decided he wanted to be alone.

Jeff Anderson was waiting for her outside the auditorium. She sailed by him without speaking. He was beneath her notice.

"Hey, I just heard. What a bummer."

She walked faster.

"What's up, Shorty? You mad?"

"Why should I be mad?" A doubting Thomas could walk by himself.

"Where you headed?"

"My locker, if you must know, and I'm in a hurry."

"Wait, I'll come with you."

Jeff trailed her down the hall and watched her put on her jacket and fill her book bag. "Where to now?"

"Home. It's late and I'm hungry." She pushed the door shut. Her locker still needed straightening.

"How about a ride? My car's outside."

"No thanks." Her smile was pure ice.

"Don't be mad, Shorty. Come on, give me a break. Please."

She hesitated. He didn't deserve her forgiveness but *please* elevated him to a higher order of subspecies. "Okay. Just don't talk. I'm not up to it."

"You'll feel better if you spill," Jeff said. They cut across the grass to the parking lot and his car.

A mile of silence was about all Arabelle could stand. For the remaining five miles, she sounded off about Mr. Atwood and how he refused to let Bonnie come back and did Jeff understand that poor Mr. Zee was a broken man and for the first time ever there would be no school play or the opportunity for a budding actress to display her talent to the world and how unfair was that!

Jeff still hadn't said a word when they pulled up in front of her house.

"You said I'd feel better. Well, I don't." His silence had lasted way too long and his *please* had worn off.

"I'm thinking, Shorty. I can't think and talk at the same time."

"If only Alice and Essie didn't have scenes together, I could play both parts. Jeff, are you listening?"

Jeff drummed his fingers on the steering wheel. "I got an idea."

"I hope it's better than dancing like a hockey player."

"Give me twenty-four hours. I'll have Bonnie back — signed, sealed, and delivered."

Arabelle stared at him in the darkness. "And just how do you propose to do that?"

"By pushing Bonnie's buttons. Bonnie and I go back a long way. She's not exactly a closed book, you know."

"What buttons, Jeff?" He'd go too far, make matters worse. There was no telling what Bonnie might do. Or Mr. Atwood.

"The less you know, the better, Peanut. I got a lot

invested in this play."

"What does that mean?"

"You'll find out. Don't worry about Bonnie. Nothing terrible is gonna happen, except you get her back."

Despite her misgivings, his words filled her with crazy hope. She wouldn't breathe them to a soul — not to Erna Sue, not to Boris, not to Chip, not even to Mr. Zee. Jeff Anderson might not be the master button-pusher that he claimed. Only time would tell.

There was no sign of Jeff the following morning. Arabelle waited by his locker, then gave up when the bell rang. By noon she still hadn't seen him and guessed he had played hooky when his button-pushing plan failed. She was not surprised.

In the cafeteria Boris and Erna Sue were deep in conversation with Chip about finding a new Alice to replace the old one. The cast and crew had joined them. The mood at the table was somber. Despite pleas and threats, Erna Sue hung tough and refused to fill in for Bonnie.

Arabelle had finished her sandwich and started on her brownie when she spotted Jeff and Bonnie at a table in the corner. He had shown up after all. She watched them with interest. Whatever Jeff was saying had Bonnie stirred up. She reminded Arabelle of a horse the way she tossed her head and showed every tooth in her mouth when she laughed. As they left the cafeteria, Jeff grinned at her over Bonnie's shoulder. Did that mean victory for a button-pusher, or was Jeff just being Jeff? Her anxiety mounted until the final bell of the day.

"Rehearsal in fifteen minutes," Chip yelled on his way by.

"What's going on?"

"Bonnie's back."

Arabelle sprinted down the hall to her locker. Jeff was there, a grin plastered across his face.

"Figured you'd come."

"Is it true, Jeff?"

"Yep. Signed, sealed, and delivered. Told you."

He deserved a medal. She would never doubt him again. "How'd you do it?"

"Promise not to blab?"

"I promise."

Jeff walked with her to the auditorium. "Have you heard about the movie being filmed in Albany?"

"The one about blues or something?"

"That's the one. *Losin' the Blues at Glenwood High.* The movie needs extras — chicks like Bonnie and jocks like me to carry the spears."

"How do you know, Jeff?"

"It's on the internet. I told Bonnie that talent scouts check out school plays. Blonds like her have an edge." Jeff treated Arabelle to a lifted eyebrow, the one he wowed girls with. "I prefer dark-haired peanuts, myself."

"I'm thrilled," she replied, poker-faced.

"Figured you'd be. I told Bonnie she was blowing a chance to appear in a big movie. With her looks, she'd probably land a bit part. That really grabbed her. The more I talked, the bigger her eyes got, and they're big to begin with. She kept saying, 'You really think so?' And I kept saying, 'For sure, Bonnie.'"

"Is that true? Will a talent scout be in the audience?"

"Nope."

"You are so-o-o bad, Jeff Anderson." Arabelle batted her eyes like Bonnie and forgave him for everything.

"Glad you think so, Shorty."

"But what about Mr. Atwood? He said he'd never let Bonnie return."

"When I asked her about that, Bonnie just laughed. 'Daddy does what I tell him, Jeff, darling, and Mummy does what Daddy tells her.'"

She had run out of questions. Jeff had all the bases covered. Almost. "What about the snakes?"

"Told her there wouldn't be any."

"Did Mr. Zee agree?"

"Not yet. He will."

Surely she could think of a question that would wipe the cocky grin off his face. "Does failure ever occur to you, Jeff Anderson?"

"Once in a while, Shorty. Like when I can't turn an elephant into a dancer."

She whacked him with her playbook.

"Whoa!" Jeff parried the second blow and wrapped his arms around her.

"Let go!"

"What's the magic word?"

"HOCKEY PUCK!"

Jeff laughed and tightened his hold.

"PLEASE." She flung the word at him, her smile hidden so he wouldn't see the pleasure that she found in his arms. He was still a troglodyte, undeserving of her forgiveness.

Jeff relaxed his grip. To make matters worse, the members of the cast ogled them as they trooped into the auditorium.

"Where do you think you're going?" she hissed, when Jeff followed her.

"Same place as you. Say hello to your new prompter."

"Very funny."

"I'm serious, Peanut."

"What happened to Trish?"

"She quit when she heard Bonnie wasn't coming back. I offered to take her place."

"If you say one word about elephants when I'm dancing, Jeff Anderson, I'll never speak to you again!"

"Hey, I'll be good. We're a team, Shorty. I'm your inspiration, remember?"

Really, he was too much!

. . . *The Earl of Egmond knelt at Deirdre's feet. "You are the love of my life, Deirdre. I must have you!"*

Deirdre Glendenning's eyes flashed fire. "It is impossible, sir. The stage is my husband. I will take no other."

"Renounce me, fair maid, and I will kill myself."

Deirdre Alexis Glendenning smiled pitilessly. "Do what you must, Denys Fitzroy..."

The cast gathered on stage. The first thing Bonnie did

when she joined them was eye the snake tank.

"It's empty," Chip said.

"Oh, Chippy, that's so sweet." Bonnie didn't seem the least contrite about what had happened and giggled and flirted in the old way as though the problem of snakes and her father had nothing to do with her.

Mr. Zee arrived last. "We're glad you're back, Bonnie. We're especially glad the play will come off. In deference to your phobia I've agreed to an empty snake tank lined with grass, to give the impression the tank holds snakes."

"I don't have a phobia," Bonnie simpered. "What gave you that idea?"

"I've also made a last-minute change to the cast," Mr. Zee said. "Arabelle is replacing Kyra. I expect all of you to help her out."

"But she's a ninth grader!" Bonnie cried.

Mr. Zee frowned. "Since when are ninth graders barred from school plays?" He repeated the question when Bonnie didn't answer.

Bonnie shrugged. "Since never. She could've tried out."

Arabelle opened her mouth, but quickly shut it. No matter what she said Bonnie would contradict and make her out a liar.

As Arabelle waited in the wings for her first entrance, Bonnie sidled up to her. "I hope you're a good dancer, Felix. You don't want to make a fool of yourself."

"I'll never be as good as Kyra, but I won't make a fool of myself, so don't get your hopes up."

"I don't know what you mean."

"Yes, you do. You hope I'll fall on my face. But I plan to disappoint you."

Bonnie was so pathetic. Arabelle would have laughed except for the cold fingers that suddenly wrapped themselves around her heart and wouldn't let go.

A Solemn Mission

For the rest of the week Arabelle danced on eggshells. In rehearsal, she ran on tiptoe around the dining room table and fluttered her arms. She managed arabesques by holding onto the sideboard.

Bonnie ignored her. In their scenes together, she pitched her lines to the bust of Athena on top of the sideboard; not once did she look at Arabelle.

"Bonnie, I want you to look at Arabelle when you say your lines."

"I am, Mr. Zee."

"No you're not. You're looking at Athena."

Bonnie humored him with her tinkly laugh. "Whatever you say, Mr. Zee."

They did the scene again, and this time Bonnie addressed Arabelle's collarbone. Progress!

By Thursday Bonnie was the model of good behavior. She had learned her part almost perfectly and followed Mr. Zee's directions without arguing. She stood on stage where she was supposed to and entered and exited on cue. She waited for Jeff to prompt her when she forgot a line. The rest of the cast placed bets on how long the reformed Bonnie would last.

At noon on Friday, Jeff joined Arabelle, Erna Sue, and Boris at one end of the table where the cast and crew gathered. Chip and Bonnie sat at the other end. Erna Sue, who disapproved of jocks, cross-examined Jeff.

"I've always wanted to be a prompter," Jeff insisted. "It's a dream come true."

Erna Sue gave him the fisheye. "You don't say."

"Yeah, I do. I'm not your average hockey puck, you know. I have deep a interest in the arts."

"Uh-huh."

"Honest! Boris will vouch for me."

"Da. Jeff teach Alex ballet."

"You're joking." Erna Sue squinted at Arabelle. "Is that true?"

"Of course not, but he tried." She didn't say how.

"I'll bet that was a showstopper," Erna Sue said, unable to keep a straight face.

Arabelle sighed. Another put-down to add to the growing number.

"Hey, I was brilliant!" Jeff said, to Erna Sue's amusement.

A roar of laughter erupted at the far end of the table.

One of the crew was doing an imitation of Mr. Zee rolling up his sleeves and tearing his hair out by the roots.

"*Merde!* All of you are *merde!* I am going to shoot myself!"

When Arabelle looked, Bonnie's eyes were fastened on her. Arabelle forced herself to stare back. She wondered what was going through Bonnie's mind. Maybe it was better not to know. Bonnie looked away first.

"Dress rehearsals next week," Mr. Zee announced that afternoon. "I want you in costume. Girls, that means skirts or dresses. No minis. No bare midriffs. I don't want to see one bellybutton. Boys? White shirts, ties, and jackets. No jeans, no sneakers, no piercings."

Penelope moaned. "We'll look like our parents."

"You'll look like what you're supposed to. This is an old-fashioned play. I don't want a bunch of gonzos prancing around on stage."

Mr. Zee rubbed the back of his neck, his habit at the end of a long week. "Stage crew, set looks good. You've outdone yourselves. Arabelle?"

"Right here."

"Tutu looks great. Dancing's fine. Keep it simple."
"Thanks, Mr. Zee." She loved the look and feel of the tutu when she danced. Anything was possible in a tutu this beautiful.

"You're almost as good as Kyra," Bonnie simpered. She wriggled her nose at Arabelle.

Arabelle smiled back. It was a lie, of course. She wasn't

even close to dancing like Kyra, but with greater effort she'd be closer. Practicing at home helped. Day by day she improved. Her jetés were almost gazelle-like and she'd finally managed an arabesque without landing in the wood-pile.

"Bonnie, you've worked hard," Mr. Zee said. "I'm proud of you. All of you have worked hard, and it shows." Mr. Zee beamed at them. His praise was so worth the wait. "I don't want you to let down between now and next Friday. Any questions?"

"What about makeup, Mr. Zee?"

"Girls, apply your own war paint. Boys, you won't need much. Costume and makeup rehearsal next Tuesday, full rehearsals Wednesday and Thursday. On Friday I want everyone here an hour ahead of curtain time. Questions?"

There were none.

The next morning, on her ride to Heavenly Rest, Arabelle practiced her speech to Happy about opening night. Of course, she might not need a speech. Hadn't Happy told her not to worry? Surely Happy understood that with Mrs. Becker in the audience reciting Essie's lines, Arabelle would draw a blank. Mr. Wexler wouldn't help matters, either. Nor would Mr. Huckabee, unless he wore his hearing aids. If she had to, she would offer Mr. Rosen as the best reason not to come. The success of the play and her performance depended on it.

She had started again on her speech when she spotted someone in the distance coming toward her. At first she paid no attention. Head down, hunched over the handle-bars, she barely looked up when she pedaled by the figure on foot. The next minute she skidded to a stop.

The old man on the opposite side of the road hurried by, without a wave or a smile or the slightest sign that he had seen her. He carried a bundle.

"Mr. Wexler, wait!" she yelled. He ignored her.

She waited for a moving van and an oil truck to pass by before she crossed over to his side. In the distance she saw him turn off the road and disappear into the woods.

"Hold on, Mr. Wexler!" she shouted.

Where in the world was he going? She had to catch him before he hurt himself or lost his way. Terrible things happened to old people when they wandered.

The weatherworn sign where Mr. Wexler turned off said Old Forge Trail, the trail the Wexlers were hiking when Mrs. Wexler died. It was a trail Arabelle knew well. She shoved her bike under a clump of juniper and took off after Mr. Wexler.

"You shouldn't be out here," she said, when she caught up with him. "Does Happy know?"

She followed in his wake asking the same question over and over, "Where are you going?"

"Help me! Help me!" he said every time she asked.

At a point farther along, he struck out on a path that led away from the main trail. Mr. Wexler was a man on a mission.

Arabelle heard the sound of rushing water well before Mr. Wexler led them into a clearing at the end of the path.

A stream swollen by autumn rain tumbled over rocks and boulders to form a shallow pool with a pebbly bottom before it dropped away in rapid falls. She knew where she was without being told. What she didn't know was why they were there.

Mr. Wexler sat on a log and removed his shoes.

"It's too cold to wade, Mr. Wexler. Please put your shoes on. We have to go back. Happy will be worried." Off came the socks. "Please don't, Mr. Wexler." When he started to roll up his pants, she stopped his hands and forced him to look at her. "I'm calling Happy. I don't care if you want me to or not." She dug for her cell phone and showed it to him. He needed to know she meant business. "I'm calling, okay?"

A stern voice answered after the first ring. "Miss Holliday is out on the grounds. Please call back."

"Is she hunting for Mr. Wexler?"

"I'm sorry, that's privileged information."

"Please tell Happy that I'm with Mr. Wexler. We're on the Old Forge Trail. Ask her to send the Heavenly Rest van for us."

During the call, Arabelle watched Mr. Wexler untie the bundle that he had brought with him. The unwrapping was done tenderly, in reverence, as if the contents were sacred relics. What Arabelle saw instead was a heap of fine sand in shades of gray and white and small chunks of rock. Head bent, Mr. Wexler brooded over his treasure.

"Time to go back," she said in a brisk, cheerful voice. To her dismay, he took a handful of the sand and rock and picked his way barefoot to the edge of the stream.

"What're you doing, Mr. Wexler?" She couldn't imagine why he dribbled sand and rocks into a rushing stream. He returned to his bundle and for the first time she saw tears glistening on his cheeks.

"Help me, help me." He held out his fist.

Arabelle cupped her hands to receive the mysterious offering, then drew back as the terrible truth dawned. Up close the sand was more like ash and what she thought were rocks weren't rocks at all.

"Is this Mrs. Wexler?" she cried, horrified. Please, please, let this not be Mrs. Wexler.

Mr. Wexler nodded and made another journey to the stream's edge. Panicked, Arabelle ran after him. "How can you do this to her? We've got to get her back." She grabbed hold of Mr. Wexler's sleeve, but not in time. Another handful of Mrs. Wexler slipped through his fingers and sank to the bottom of the pool. Some of the larger pieces bobbed and swirled in the eddying water before they tumbled over the rocks and were swept downstream.

Mr. Wexler brushed away tears. "Help me —" He broke off. His lips moved but no sound came out.

"What is it, Mr. Wexler?" She touched his arm. "Try to tell me."

"Help me," he whispered.

"You can do it. I know you can." She waited.

"Help me."

"Happy told me this is where — where Mrs. Wexler had a heart attack." She couldn't say died. It was too final.

He fiddled with the edges of his bundle.

"Was this her favorite place?" Arabelle asked gently.

Mr. Wexler nodded, his eyes on the swirling water.

"That's why you put her in the brook, isn't it? You knew that's where she'd want to be." He nodded again.

She hadn't thought about this before, but wasn't a stream running through the woods where she'd want to be if she were dead? Certainly not in an urn or a hole in the ground.

She held out her hands, palms up. Working together, they committed the rest of Mrs. Wexler to her final resting place. Arabelle marveled that there was so little of a grown person in death.

"Was she small like me, Mr. Wexler?"

He smiled and showed her how tall. She and Mrs. Wexler were the same height.

"We should be going," she said, after the last handful of ash sank from sight. "Happy's sending the van for us."

Mr. Wexler sat down on the bank. His eyes pled for more time.

Arabelle knelt beside him. "Oh, how I wish you could talk — really talk. Sometimes I know what you mean, but a lot of the time I don't. I have to guess."

They watched the moving stream in silence. Mr. Wexler seemed content to sit quietly with his memories. Arabelle drew her knees up under her chin and stared at the water. She had no idea where her grandpa was buried. It hadn't occurred to her to ask. A stream in the woods had changed that.

"My grandfather had a heart attack," she said in an undertone. "He was in a nursing home. I hardly ever talk about it."

Mr. Wexler reached for her hand.

"My mom thinks I don't remember, but I do. Until Heavenly Rest I hated nursing homes. Grandpa died in his. He fell out of his wheelchair and died in the hall. No one could save him." At first she hadn't understood what was happening. Her wonderful grandpa lay on the floor with lots of people pushing on his chest. Someone put a funny-looking cup over his nose and mouth that she later learned was an oxygen mask. She remembered crying and holding tight to her mother's hand.

"I thought I had killed him," she said. There, it was out. She had never before uttered that terrible thought out loud.

"Help me! Help me!" Mr. Wexler cried, shaking his head.

She went on, unable to stop. "I liked to sit on my grandpa's lap. I was five. We'd race up and down the hall in his wheelchair and toot make-believe horns at imaginary pedestrians and traffic. He had a pain and wanted to stop. If I hadn't begged him for one more ride, he'd have lived." Mr. Wexler grabbed both her hands. Never! She mustn't think that. She was wrong. She had not killed him. All this she read in his eyes; words weren't needed.

"Probably I didn't," she said, grateful for his certainty, "but I'm glad I told you and that you understand." She traced the blue veins on the back of his hand with her finger. He must be very old. Her grandpa had had blue veins, too. "Do you have grandchildren, Mr. Wexler?"

He shook his head.

Did she dare ask him? What if he said no? She banished the thought at once. "How would you like to be my grandpa?"

He gave her fingers a gentle squeeze. "Help me, help me."

Arabelle had no trouble understanding the answer or his joy that she had asked. As they sat together, hand in hand, Arabelle felt grateful for this moment in a place they both loved. The wind sighed in the branches overhead.

Although she wanted to, she couldn't quite bring herself to invite him to the play. Her fear that he'd cry out was too great. Maybe if he sat in the back row, only the people closest to him would be disturbed. But if he came, so would the rest of them, and everyone in the auditorium would hear Mrs. Becker and Mr. Huckabee no matter where they sat. If only there was a way. But she couldn't think of one.

"Time to go, Grandpa." She handed him his socks and shoes and helped him to his feet. Then they headed down the trail. This time Arabelle led.

The van pulled up just as they arrived at the trailhead. The driver stowed her bike in back. She and Mr. Wexler sat side by side for the short ride to Heavenly Rest.

Happy was waiting for them by the front door. "Merciful heaven, you're back. What a miracle! Lana, take Mr. Wexler to his room. He could use a little wash-up before lunch."

"Help me! Help me!" Mr. Wexler called as Lana steered him past the reception desk and through the double doors.

"Lana, wait." Arabelle overtook them. She reached up and kissed Mr. Wexler on the cheek. "I'll see you soon, Grandpa. May I tell Happy what we were doing?"

"Help me," he said in a husky voice and kissed her on the brow.

Arabelle heard the dinner gong sound in the distance. She had Happy's ear and five precious minutes to deliver her speech. But first she told Happy what Mr. Wexler had done with Mrs. Wexler and why, which took longer than she intended. She dove in just as the gong sounded for the second time.

"About opening night, Happy —"

"I'm so glad you brought that up. Mrs. Becker found a copy of the play in our library. Isn't she the one! She reads it aloud to the group every morning after sing along. They can't wait to see you perform."

"But — but you said not to worry. I thought that meant — that you meant — oh, I don't know what I thought."

"I was sure they'd forget about the play, Arabelle, but that's all they talk about. You're the biggest excitement they've had in years." Happy patted her hand. "They'll be good as gold, I promise. "

The only way that would happen was if they were bound and gagged. Maybe she could convince Mr. Zee to seat them in the last row of the auditorium, where they wouldn't see or hear very much. Or maybe she'd tell them that every seat in the house was sold.

The thought of deceiving them shamed her. How could she do that to her friends, especially friends who cared for her as much as they did? Why had she told them about the play in the first place? Why hadn't she let them believe she was having a baby?

Meltdown

The next morning, Arabelle called Erna Sue. "I have a surprise and a problem. Okay if I come over?"

"What's your surprise?"

"I can't tell you. I have to show you."

"Why can't we meet at your house?"

"Because I need a big living room."

"You'll have to be careful. My mother doesn't like anyone on her rug." The Comstocks had recently completed a major renovation to their downstairs.

When a short time later Arabelle stood in Erna Sue's front hall, she said, "Do we have permission from on high?" What was the point of a rug you couldn't walk on?

"I didn't ask. The parents are out."

Erna Sue made Arabelle remove her shoes before they stepped into the living room. The pale yellow rug and marble-top tables reminded Arabelle of a hotel lobby.

"So what do you want to show me, Alex?"

"In a sec. First we need to brainstorm. My friends at Heavenly Rest want to come to the play. I don't know how to stop them. They'll ruin everything." She lay back on the rug, confident that Erna Sue would have a solution.

"Tell Happy they can't. Tell her they won't understand it."

"But they do. Mrs. Becker reads from the play every morning and explains each scene."

"I'll speak to Mr. Zee, Alex. He'll figure something out."

Arabelle smiled her thanks. The problem was as good as solved.

The doorbell rang and Erna Sue went to answer it. A minute later Jeff and Boris bounded into the room.

"Stop! Shoes off!" Erna Sue ordered.

Arabelle sat up. "What are you two doing here?"

"Your mom told us where you were," Jeff said. "We thought we'd drop by and make your day."

"Da. Jeff call me. He want company. We fool around in car."

"That's tool around, buddy."

Erna Sue carried their shoes like roadkill to the front hall. "Since you're here," she said when she returned, " — not that you were invited — Alex has a surprise."

Arabelle had counted on surprising Erna Sue in private. But with so much at stake, she couldn't back out now. "I'm a far better dancer than what you've seen in rehearsals," she began. "I've been taking ballet lessons."

Erna Sue's mouth fell open. "Who with?"

Arabelle hesitated. "Maria Tallchief."

"Isn't she dead?"

Arabelle had no idea. "I don't think so. Is she?"

"Who's Maria Tallchief?" Jeff asked.

"She Russian dancer."

"She's Native American," Erna Sue said. "You're taking lessons online, aren't you, Alex?"

"From a DVD. The lessons follow *Swan Lake*. My jetés have improved and I can almost do an arabesque without holding on."

"Does Mr. Zee know?" Erna Sue asked.

"I want to surprise him."

"I wouldn't do that, Alex. Mr. Zee likes how you dance."

"But I don't like how I dance. Kyra was much better than me."

"Let us be the judge," Erna Sue said.

"Show us what you got, Shorty." Jeff stretched out on Mrs. Comstock's rug. Boris did the same. No one wanted to sit on the furniture.

"Be careful of the lamps, Alex," Erna Sue cautioned.

Arabelle started at one end of the living room and without stopping jetéd to the other end. She swung her arms the way Maria did when she jetéd.

"Was I okay?" Arabelle asked, when no one clapped or said a word.

"Da. Is good."

Arabelle blew Boris a kiss. "How was I, Jeff?"

"So-so."

"Boris liked me."

"He's being polite."

Arabelle eyed them in disbelief. How could they not like her jetés after her hours of practice and self-sacrifice? She looked at Erna Sue. "What do you think?"

"You're supposed to hold onto the furniture, Alex. That's what Mr. Zee wants."

"Essie doesn't hold onto anything, Erna Sue. Nowhere in the stage directions does Essie hold on."

"What else you got, Peanut?"

"An arabesque. You probably won't like that either." She lifted her leg behind her and flung both arms over her head. "Oops!" On her way down, she barely missed a vase of silk orchids on the coffee table.

"That wasn't so good. My pirouette is much, much better. Watch this." With her arms curved in front of her, Arabelle twirled slowly on the balls of both feet. "How was that?"

"Needs work," Jeff said.

"Da."

She didn't bother to ask Erna Sue.

"I wish I could show you my glissade. My glissades are awesome."

"So show us," Jeff said.

"I can't on a rug. It's a skating step." She flopped down on the damask sofa.

Erna Sue jumped up. "Watch the upholstery!"

Arabelle slid to the floor, defeated by Mrs. Comstock's living room and a poor showing in front of her friends. Her voice trembled. "I'm so much better than what you've seen."

"You're too old for ballet," Erna Sue said. "You should've started younger."

Arabelle glared at Jeff, who lay on his back grinning at the ceiling. "I suppose you agree."

"Give it a rest, Shorty. If I played hockey the way you dance —"

"You'd be less of a jerk!"

Jeff hitched up on his elbows. "Easy, Peanut. I was just kidding."

"Don't call me Peanut! My name is Arabelle and I don't speak to clueless jerks in love with themselves."

Jeff turned brick red. "Fine by me."

"True friends encourage you," Arabelle cried. "True friends tell you not to give up. True friends are sometimes wrong!"

"True friends tell you the truth," Erna Sue snapped. "True friends don't want you to fall on your face opening night."

Arabelle grabbed her coat and stalked from the living room. Erna Sue trailed her to the front door.

"We're only trying to help, Alex."

Arabelle shoved her feet into her waterproof hikers without untying them. "I'm sorry I came over. I'm sorry I danced for you. I'm sorry we were ever friends."

Erna Sue drew back as though she had been slapped.

"I'm sorry — I didn't mean —" Arabelle reached out a hand.

Erna Sue swatted it away. "I don't need your friendship, Alex. I have plenty of friends who appreciate and respect me for what I am. Friends who matter." She held the door open, her eyes averted, but not in time to hide her tears.

"I didn't mean it," Arabelle muttered to herself on the way home. How could Erna Sue believe she did? Erna Sue should know better. Hadn't they been friends for two years going on three? Now that she thought back, not once had she ever seen Erna Sue cry, not even when they had their fight over Mrs. Cushman. This fight was no different. By tomorrow Erna Sue would come to her senses. "That's okay, Alex," she'd say, "I know you didn't mean it," and they'd laugh and be back to normal. She'd apologize to Jeff and crack a joke, and he'd laugh and tell her that she wasn't that bad a dancer and ask her forgiveness.

On opening night she would show them both what she was made of, once and for all.

The next day at lunch, Arabelle addressed all of her remarks to Erna Sue. Erna Sue addressed all of her remarks to Boris. When Arabelle offered to get rid of Erna Sue's tray along with her own, she got a frosty "No, thank you," and not so much as a glance.

"What wrong?" Boris asked, after Erna Sue had left.

Arabelle was ashamed to tell him. "I hurt her feelings. I said something I shouldn't have."

"What you say?"

"That I was sorry we were friends. I told her I didn't mean it, but she won't make up."

"She no stay mad," Boris assured her. "Not her nature."

Arabelle wanted to believe him, just as she wanted to believe that Jeff would forgive her and they'd be friends again and he wouldn't eat at the hockey table for the rest of the week, or maybe longer, with his back to her.

Tuesday afternoon the cast turned out in costume. One by one, Mr. Zee checked their clothing, hair, and makeup.

"Skirt's too tight, Alice. Get rid of the false eyelashes."

"But my lashes aren't long enough, Mr. Zee."

"You heard me. Tony, find another tie, please. Yours barks." Chip laughed and stripped off his Day-Glo tie.

"Gay, a little heavier on the makeup, Penelope, a little lighter. Grandpa, you need a pocket watch and chain. Check with wardrobe. Kirbys, I want you in evening clothes. See me afterwards. Kolenkhov, you don't look Russian enough. See if wardrobe has a beret and a string tie."

The Grand Duchess Olga Katrina, tricked out in a fur stole and swinging a pearl necklace that hung to her waist, did a bump and grind around the stage. The cast laughed and applauded.

Arabelle was last up for inspection. She flitted to the front of the stage and curtsied.

"Mr. Zee, don't you think Essie's costume is a little

too revealing?" Bonnie asked. Her eyes couldn't have been wider or more innocent if she tried.

"I wear tights, Bonnie, in case you haven't noticed."

"Oh, do you? Silly me."

"Essie's costume is fine," Mr. Zee said. "I don't want to hear a word against it."

Tuesday's rehearsal stopped frequently for last-minute adjustments. Act two went badly. The couch collapsed and needed emergency repairs after Gay passed out one too many times. In his dance scene with Essie, Kolenkhov couldn't take his shirt off when it caught in his zipper. The rehearsal ground to a halt while Boris took care of the matter backstage. Halfway through act three, Bonnie started screaming. Someone had put a rubber hose in the snake tank. It took ten minutes for Chip and Mr. Zee to calm her down. Mr. Zee threatened expulsion and jail time if it happened again.

Wednesday was no improvement on Tuesday.

At lunch Erna Sue walked right by the empty seat next to Arabelle and set her tray down at the far end of the table. Arabelle waited for her to finish and leave. They crossed paths by the tray rack.

"Hi, Erna Sue." Arabelle tried in vain to catch her eye.

"Hi." Erna Sue stowed the remains of her lunch and headed for the door.

Arabelle watched her go. At least Erna Sue had spoken. She waited by the door for Jeff, her speech ready. Jeff, surrounded by his hockey mates, nodded to her on his way out. She watched him go, the breath sucked out of her.

In rehearsal that afternoon, Bonnie forgot her lines and ad-libbed.

"How can she know her lines one day and forget them the next?" Arabelle complained under her breath.

"That's how she calls attention to herself," Lizbeth said. Twice Arabelle caught Jeff looking at her, but despite her efforts he kept his distance.

On Thursday Arabelle confronted Erna Sue in the hall. "I didn't mean what I said. Please don't be mad."

Erna Sue stared over Arabelle's shoulder. "I'm late for class, Alex." Arabelle stepped aside to let her pass, her plea for mercy denied. Trying harder didn't work. It made matters worse. She had taken forgiveness for granted and Erna Sue was getting even.

Helpless and tongue-tied, Arabelle watched Jeff go by with Kiki and the wraparounds. In the space of one week, she was back to non-personhood, abandoned by her friends and rock bottom in the pecking order. After tomorrow night, she'd ask her parents to homeschool her. She would finish ninth grade in the silence of her lonely room.

The final rehearsal on Friday dragged. "You're putting me to sleep," Mr. Zee yelled. "Pick up the pace." In the first act, Grandpa dried up in the middle of his heart-to-heart with God. "Grandpa needs a prompt. Jeff, where are you?" Jeff poked his head around the curtain. "Sorry, sir." The G-men made their entrance too early and ruined the end of act two. They repeated the scene several times before

Mr. Zee was satisfied. At the conclusion of act three the Grand Duchess carried a plate of blintzes from the kitchen and tripped. The blintzes went flying. They did the scene over.

"It's still not right," Mr. Zee said. "We don't go home 'til it's right."

In despair, Arabelle wondered how the play could possibly open the following night, or ever.

Ready or Not!

Arabelle was wide awake when her alarm went off the next morning. She had spent the most awful night. In her first dream she stood on stage stark naked. In her second dream she had clothes on but she didn't know her lines. Toward dawn she dreamed that snakes were in her bed and woke screaming.

Mr. Zee had not canceled the play or postponed opening night. For better or for worse, she would don Kyra's tutu, lace up her slippers, and hope for the best. She hadn't expected jitters this early in the day. She had expected to be nervous, but not so short of breath or paralyzed at the thought of dancing in front of an audience.

She skipped breakfast. "I'd throw up on the bus," she told her mother. "Don't wait dinner for me. I won't be home after school."

"Sweetie, you should eat."

"I will, Mom, don't worry." She'd eat a little extra at lunch to tide her over.

In homeroom, Arabelle practiced her lines, moving her lips in silent repetition as she put words together with dance in her head. When the bell rang, she had completed act one without forgetting a line or falling down.

In English, she tuned out and started act two. Her English teacher rarely called on her.

She had just begun her ballet lesson with Kolenkhov when she heard her name.

"Essie Carmichael," she stammered, bewildered by her teacher's stern question, which she hadn't expected or heard. The class tittered. "I'm sorry. What are we talking about?"

"We are discussing *As You Like It*, Arabelle, which apparently you haven't read."

"Yes, I have. I didn't hear the question. Could you repeat it?"

"Orlando. Who does Orlando love?"

She couldn't quite remember. It was an R name. Roxanne? Rosamund?

"Rosalind, Arabelle."

"That's what I was about to say. Orlando didn't want to live until he met her." She threw that in to prove she had done the assignment.

"Perhaps you might read more carefully in the future, Arabelle."

She paid close attention for the rest of the period.

"I can't be in this play. I have terminal stage fright," she told Boris after class.

"Everybody get stage fright. Go out, say lines, stage fright go away."

"But what if I forget them? Not just one or two, but all of them?"

"Jeff help you."

"He's not speaking to me. He'll let me twist in the wind."

Boris looked puzzled. "What means?"

"When you hang by a rope, your body twists around and around."

"Jeff no let you hang. He cut you down."

Boris could think what he liked. She knew better.

The rest of the morning crawled by. At noon Arabelle waited her turn in the lunch line. She noticed Erna Sue and Boris sitting together, their backs to her, and opposite them for the first time that week, Jeff. The cast and crew occupied all the other seats at the table.

Quite by chance, Jeff looked up and their eyes met. A week ago she'd have waved at him and he'd have clowned back. A week ago Erna Sue would have saved her a seat. If only Boris would turn around and see her. Today of all days she needed a friend who wasn't mad at her. Arabelle replaced her tray and ducked out the door. There was no room for her at that table. She would make do with peanut butter crackers and a Coke from the vending machines.

She carried her lunch to the auditorium and sat in the

last row, glad for the semi-darkness. If anyone wandered in, she wouldn't be noticed. As she nibbled her crackers, she peered at the dimly lit stage. Her friends from Heavenly Rest wouldn't see much this far back. Grandpa Wexler might miss her altogether if the people in front of him blocked his view. She fretted over the possibility. He would never forgive her. None of them would. But any closer and they'd ruin the play.

Arabelle drained the last of her Coke and stopped by the nurse's office on her way to History. "I don't feel well," she said. "I think I'm coming down with something."

The nurse popped a thermometer in Arabelle's mouth and took her pulse. "Temperature's normal," she said. "Pulse is a bit rapid, but at your age that's not unusual." The nurse gave her a cheery smile and an aspirin, which Arabelle tossed into the drinking fountain. She'd need more than aspirin to get through the afternoon.

At three o'clock, she went to her locker, put on her jacket, and headed outside to the athletic field. A chill wind hinting of snow sprang up as she sat on the bleachers reciting her lines. She hadn't been there long before a figure, clad in sweats and a warm-up jacket, suddenly appeared across the field. It was Jeff.

She watched him loosen up with leg stretches and take a swig from his water bottle, and she followed his measured progress as he jogged around the track. When he drew closer, she stopped reciting. Maybe he'd see her and stop.

The wind tore at her heart when he jogged by without

a glance. She jumped to her feet and ran after him. "Jeff, wait!"

He kept going. Maybe he hadn't heard her. She yelled "Jeff!" again before he stopped and turned around. She had the worst pain in her side and no idea what to say to him. They stared at each other.

"What're you doing out here?" he asked, jogging in place.

"Trying to freeze to death before tonight." She hoped he'd smile at the silliness.

"Don't let me stop you," he said, his stare as flat as his voice.

Arabelle shivered in the cold. He didn't care whether she lived or died. "I'm so nervous," she babbled. "What if I forget my lines?" Anything to keep him longer.

"You won't."

Her pulse quickened. He still believed in her.

Jeff regarded her coolly. "Jog around the track. You'll feel better."

The pain in her side had spread to her stomach. "Okay if I run with you?"

"I'd have to slow down. You'll do better on your own."

He was paying her back. Hadn't she said, 'I'll do better on my own,' none too nicely, when he had tried to help her dance?

She couldn't think of another thing to say except what no one ever wanted to hear. "I think I'm going to be sick." She stumbled off the track and made it to the grass just as the remains of the peanut butter crackers and Coke parted company with her stomach.

Jeff ambled over. "You all right?"

"I think so." This was the last straw. She had made a complete fool of herself by throwing up. "I wish you hadn't seen."

Jeff handed her his water bottle. "The hockey team always barfs before big games. One guy never makes it to the bathroom."

He was trying to make her feel better. She loved him for that. With a little more effort on her part, he might love her back. She rinsed her mouth and handed him the bottle.

Jeff backed away. "You can keep it." He jogged off without another word.

Holding her side, she half-ran, half-jogged after him. She refused to be brushed off so easily.

Jeff reached the starting point on the track first. "Are you still here?" he asked when she caught up with him.

The ultimate put-down. Once again she had tried too hard. "Don't worry, I'm leaving. Sorry I bothered you."

He slung a towel around his neck. "Where are you going, Arabelle?"

"Inside, where I won't bug you!" She longed for him to call her Shorty, but those days were over.

"Better cool down or you'll cramp." The captain of the hockey team was all business.

She let him lead her in stretches and bends, and didn't mind when he chewed her out for not touching her toes. She existed; she was one of the guys. After several hamstring exercises Jeff called a halt. "Feeling better?"

"Yes, thanks. The stretches helped." They shared an awkward silence.

"Drink plenty of water and eat light, Arabelle. You can pig out after the show."

She left him doing pushups and went straight to the girls' locker room. Never had a hot shower felt so good. She stood under the nozzle for a long time. At home when she did this, her parents banged on the door and told her to turn the water off. Afterwards she got a lecture about drought in Africa and how her single shower consumed enough water to irrigate Chad.

Eat light and drink plenty of water, Jeff had said, and since she was prepared to follow his advice because he hadn't quite given up on her, she headed for the vending machines outside the cafeteria. Three bottles of water and two power bars would have to sustain her through the next several hours.

The girls' dressing room buzzed with nervous energy and bursts of laughter. An hour to curtain time and everyone was full of adrenalin.

A dressing table ran the full length of the room. Scattered on top were jars of grease paint, a collection of eyebrow pencils, lipsticks in shades of red, hair pieces, and false eyelashes. Above the table hung three large mirrors rimmed with bright lights that revealed every zit, including ones that weren't there but soon would be. Bonnie, running her mouth, hogged the middle mirror while she applied eyeliner and two pounds of mascara to her lashes.

"Guess who'll be in the audience?" she twittered. "A Hollywood talent scout. Jeff says they check out school plays . . ."

Smiling to herself, Arabelle donned leotard and tights and slipped into Kyra's tutu. Her ballet slippers came next, then her hair, which she tied in a ponytail with a pink ribbon.

". . . He'll want to give me a screen test, that's what Jeff said. Jeff says blonds have an edge. I'll probably land a small part —"

"Bonnie, shut up!" Lizbeth snapped. "I need to say my lines."

"Well, if you don't know them by now —" Bonnie stopped short when she met Lizbeth's eyes in the mirror. Since the incident of the snakes, Bonnie treated Lizbeth with extreme caution.

Silence gathered in the dressing room. Reflected in the mirrors were six faces in various stages of transformation. Lips moved soundlessly as lines were recited over and over so none would be forgotten. Soon trips to the bathroom started. Arabelle noted with satisfaction that Bonnie went twice in fifteen minutes.

At 7:45 Erna Sue stuck her head in the door. "Mr. Zee wants everyone on stage."

The cast crowded around Mr. Zee as he perched on the dining room table. The rising tide of voices and laughter beyond the closed curtain promised a full house.

"Are we all here?" Mr. Zee spoke quietly so he wouldn't

be heard out front. "I want you to have fun tonight. That's what putting on a play is all about. If you have fun, the audience has fun. Don't worry if you flub a line. Even the best actors flub lines. Just keep going. When the audience laughs, let 'em laugh before you say your next line. Don't slack off between acts. Keep the energy up." Mr. Zee beamed at the anxious faces around him. "Break a leg, gang!"

Arabelle peeked through a chink in the curtain, her heart racing. Except for the front row, the auditorium was packed. She spotted her parents halfway back. Her father was reading one of his science journals to pass the time and her mother chatted with the woman next to her. Her eye traveled to the back rows. The seats were filled but not with her friends from Heavenly Rest. She scanned the middle rows. They hadn't come after all, and it was her fault. Why had she told them not to? She should have insisted they come. They were the only friends she had.

A sudden flurry in back of the auditorium caught her eye.

"Omigosh," Arabelle whispered. Happy and Lana were guiding walkers and wheelchairs through the rear door. A student usher signaled them to follow.

Please, please no closer, she prayed the farther down the aisle they came. She watched, transfixed, as they settled into their seats, where she didn't want them to be. In the front row! Practically on stage! Close enough to touch!

Grandpa Wexler, wearing a navy blazer and a red tie, held a bouquet of yellow mums on his lap. Mrs. Becker, decked out in a bright pink pantsuit and a green feather boa that only she would wear, sat beside Gwenda, the playbook on her lap. Lana sat next to Gwenda and Happy next to Mr. Rosen. Arabelle couldn't tell what he had on under his jacket. Mr. Huckabee, hunched in his wheelchair, scowled at the program and fiddled with his ear.

"Come away from the curtain, Arabelle," Mr. Zee said. She grabbed his sleeve. "Did Erna Sue mention my friends from Heavenly Rest?"

"She thought they should sit in the back. I told the ushers to seat them up front. Elderly people need to be able to see and hear."

"You don't understand," she gibbered. "They'll talk out loud and ruin everything. Grandpa — Mr. Wexler cries for help constantly. Mrs. Becker recites lines. Mr. Huckabee will shout at us to speak up."

Mr. Zee took hold of her shoulders. "Calm down, Arabelle. Remember what I told you? Steady as she goes."

"Like the Queen Mary."

"That's right. Your friends are here to cheer you on. If they're a little noisy, raise your voice. An actor controls the audience, not the other way around."

"But —"

"No buts, Arabelle."

He didn't understand and wouldn't until it was too late. The Queen Mary was headed straight for an iceberg. The ship and all hands were doomed.

"Places," Mr. Zee called softly.

The actors for the first scene gathered in the wings.

Arabelle waited, fidgeting, for the stage lights to come up, her hands clenched and sweaty, her throat as dry as sandpaper. The curtain rose slowly on Penelope Sycamore seated at her typewriter.

"You're on," Jeff whispered.

Arabelle fluttered from the wings, fanning herself, since the day was very hot and she had just come from a steamy kitchen.

Somehow she recited her lines without forgetting any, and Penelope said her lines back and only forgot once, and by some miracle Arabelle accomplished an arabesque holding onto the sideboard. The audience laughed and applauded.

From time to time Arabelle snuck peeks at the front row. So far Grandpa Wexler hadn't uttered one cry for help, and though Mrs. Becker leaned forward and moved her lips, not a sound came out. Twice Arabelle caught Mr. Huckabee laughing. He must have put his hearing aids in. Mr. Rosen and what he wore under his jacket remained a major worry.

Every time Arabelle danced, the audience clapped. She began to relax. Everything would be fine. She could do this. She and Essie Carmichael were made for each other.

The perfect moment to show off her newfound skill came in the final scene of act one. While the cast looked on in confusion, Arabelle whirled and jetéd around the set like Maria Tallchief, narrowly missing the xylophone and Penelope's typing chair. Unassisted by furniture, she ended with an arabesque and teetered off-balance, windmilling her arms to stay upright. The audience loved it. When the curtain fell, Arabelle danced into the wings. She had received the most laughs and the most applause. Her hours of practice had paid off.

Chip tugged her ponytail in passing. "You were terrific, Alex."

"Thanks, Chip. So were you."

She ignored Bonnie who swept by, clipping her. "Oops, so sorry, Essie. I didn't see you." Bonnie flashed a phony smile. She had not been applauded.

Mr. Zee barred Arabelle's way. "What did I tell you?" She froze.

"What did I tell you?" He glowered at her.

"To — to fake it."

"You could've fallen."

"I thought you'd be pleased. I did it for you, Mr. Zee."

"No, you didn't. You did it for yourself. For the last time, Arabelle, no pirouettes, jetés, or arabesques that we haven't rehearsed. Do you understand?"

"I was only trying my best." He had seen through her.

"Know your limitations. Don't try to be something you're not."

"Yes, Mr. Zee."

"Don't make me sorry I cast you as Essie."

She gaped at him as the weight of his words sunk in. Mr. Zee must never, ever have any regrets. From now on she would dance the way he wanted and abandon all thoughts of Maria Tallchief and a standing ovation.

Act two began as Gay Wellington staggered around the stage swigging from a gin bottle. When she gazed, open-mouthed, at the snake tank and said, "'When I see snakes it's time to lay down,'" she got the biggest laugh so far.

Arabelle, on stage for most of the act, noticed that Bonnie took forever when she exited up the hall stairs. Before she disappeared from sight, she turned and waved and blew kisses, which she'd never done in rehearsals because Mr. Zee would have killed her. Arabelle guessed that the waves and kisses were for the benefit of the talent scout.

When the time came for their big dance scene, Arabelle and Boris took center stage.

"'We have a hot night for it, my Pavlova,'" Boris cried in his Kolenkhov voice, "'but art is only achieved through perspiration.'"

Arabelle waited for him to strip off his shirt and bare his chest for the sake of art. He was rewarded with applause and wolf whistles.

Kolenkhov cast a critical eye at Essie. "'You are ready? We begin.'" He signaled Ed Carmichael at the xylophone. The music started up. Kolenkhov shouted out the dance steps.

"'Pirouette!'"

Arabelle spun around on the toes of one foot, wobbling a little at the end.

The audience laughed.

"'Entrechat! Entrechat!'"

Arabelle jumped up and down. She did not cross and

uncross her ankles like Maria.

"'Pirouette!'"

This time she twirled on both feet, the way Mr. Zee wanted, and was applauded.

Thrilled, Arabelle ran on tiptoes around the dining room table, her ponytail flicking from side to side. She had started on her second circuit when, suddenly, right in her path, a foot poked out from beneath the doorway drape. Caught by surprise, unable to stop, she tripped and pitched headlong, landing in a sprawl of arms and legs, the wind knocked out of her.

The audience started to laugh and clap, then fell silent as she struggled to her knees gasping for breath. The floor beneath her rocked and swayed. Grandpa Wexler's "Help me! Help me!" and Mr. Huckabee's "What's wrong with Clarabelle?" exceeded her worst nightmare. The play lay in ruins, and through no fault of her own, she was to blame.

Reunion

Boris reached Arabelle in one stride and helped her up. "Is okay, Alex," he whispered, "don't cry."

"I can't help it." She choked back a sob.

Jeff had sprung to his feet and was practically on stage. "Do the fall again, Shorty," he called softly. "Pretend the falls are part of the act."

"Da, Jeff right," Boris murmured. "'Come, come!'" he shouted in his Kolenkhov voice. "'You can do that! It's eight years now! At last! Entrechat! Entrechat!'"

Arabelle leapt up and down, then skittered around the dining room table, tears streaming down her cheeks while Ed banged away on the xylophone. Grandpa and Penelope stepped back to give her room. Once more she tripped and landed in a sprawl, but this time on purpose, not because of someone's foot. The audience loved it. Mrs.

Becker pumped Mr. Wexler's arm. Mr. Huckabee yelled, "Atta girl, Essie!"

Jeff urged her on. "Once more, Shorty. You're doing great."

Arabelle scrambled to her knees. He forgave her. He wanted her to succeed.

Kolenkhov shouted, "'Up, up, my little Pavlova! You can do this!'" For the third time in a row Arabelle circled the table, and down she tumbled. Boris rolled his eyes and hauled her to her feet. Jeff gave her a thumbs-up from the wings.

The applause that swept over them dried the last of her tears. She even managed a smile. But it was Jeff's praise that meant the most. His quick thinking and his belief in her had saved the play. The act continued and without a hitch.

When the curtain fell to cheers and applause, Arabelle flew to the wings and caught him around the waist. "You are the absolute best ever, Jeff Anderson." She didn't care what he thought or that she was trying too hard.

He held her close, as if she mattered. "What happened out there?"

"Someone tripped me." She knew who it was, but she couldn't prove it. Everything had happened too fast.

"It was Bonnie, wasn't it?"

"I think so. Why would she trip me, Jeff? What've I done to her?"

"You stole the spotlight, Shorty. Girls like Bonnie don't appreciate that."

Erna Sue rushed to Arabelle's side. "Alex, are you okay? I was so worried. I saw what she did —"

"I'm okay —"

"What you see?" Boris broke into their tight circle and draped his arms around Arabelle and Erna Sue.

"Bonnie." Erna Sue's eyes blazed. "I was backstage. I saw her behind that drape. I saw her stick her foot out. That's battery. You go to jail for battery —"

"Thank you for caring, Erna Sue." Arabelle's voice shook. "I don't deserve a friend like you. About what I said, please, please forgive me. I didn't mean it —"

"We had a stupid fight, Alex. Let's never have another."

"I've missed you —"

"I've missed you, too —"

"You're the best friend I have."

"You're mine, too." Erna Sue hugged Arabelle in a rare display of affection. "I'll try harder to be wrong, I promise."

Arabelle hugged back. "Don't try too hard. I'd rather you were straight with me. You tell me the truth, whether I want to hear it or not."

"I hate to break this up," Jeff said, "but we need a game plan. What're we gonna do about Bonnie?"

"Tell Mr. Zee," Boris said. "He know what to do."

Arabelle and Erna Sue agreed. Jeff said, "Wait a minute, I got a better idea." Keeping his voice low, he told Boris and Erna Sue about the fake talent scout sitting in the audience. "Instead of ratting her out, I'll tell Bonnie to stay away from Shorty or I'll ruin her chances with the scout."

"Da, that good. What you think, Erna?"

"What *do* you think?" Erna Sue still hadn't given up on Boris's English. "I vote for Jeff's idea. We keep Alex safe and wreak vengeance on a batterer." They high-fived each other to seal the deal.

Arabelle was suddenly grabbed from behind in a bear hug that threatened to end her life. "I was out front when you took that nosedive," Mr. Zee said. "Couldn't believe my eyes. What happened?"

"I tripped, Mr. Zee. I was dancing the way you wanted, but I bombed."

"No, you didn't. Your impromptu falls saved the act. By God, they saved the play."

Erna Sue nodded, agreeing. "What you did was so amazing, Alex."

Arabelle couldn't have asked for a greater compliment. "Thanks, Erna Sue, but it was Jeff's idea. I couldn't have done it without him — or Boris."

"Yeah, you could've." Jeff's smile turned her to mush. "Shorty deserves the credit, Mr. Zee. When the game counted, she played through her pain."

"Da, score big!"

Arabelle, bursting with happiness, knew she would never have better friends than these.

Mr. Zee beamed. "I'd call this a team effort — yours, Arabelle's and Boris's. I'm proud of you. Keep up the good work."

In the dressing room Arabelle was the center of attention and roundly praised for her quick thinking. Bonnie kept her distance, which was fine with Arabelle. Let Jeff deal with her.

"Places for act three, people." Erna Sue held the door open. Bonnie was first out. She ignored Erna Sue's angry stare.

Arabelle looked for Jeff as she took her place in the wings. "Where is he? We can't start without a prompter."

"He has Bonnie in a corner," Lizbeth said with a snigger. "He'd better not let Mr. Zee catch him."

"It's not what you think," Arabelle said, but she wasn't about to set Lizbeth straight.

"We're cool," Jeff murmured, sliding into his chair.

"Did Bonnie agree?" Arabelle asked.

"Had no choice. She wants to be in the movies."

For most of the third act, Arabelle and Bonnie were on stage together and off stage together. Off stage, Arabelle stuck close to Jeff. On stage, she was alert for the slightest sign that Bonnie planned to end her life once and for all, no matter what Jeff said. When the act finally ended, after the Grand Duchess had carried a plate of blintzes from the kitchen without tripping, Arabelle breathed a sigh of relief. The play was over and she was still alive.

Mr. Zee lined them up for curtain calls and told them to stay in character.

The cast took their bows two by two. When it was Arabelle's and Boris's turn, Boris planted himself center stage, hands on hips, every inch the ballet master, while

Arabelle circled him like a pollinating bee. The audience went crazy.

Mr. Wexler and Mrs. Becker jumped to their feet. "Help me!" Mr. Wexler waved his bouquet in celebration. Mrs. Becker, holding tight to his arm, yelled, "Encore, dahling, encore!"

"Well done!" Mr. Rosen called.

Mr. Huckabee shouted, "Three cheers for Clarabelle!"

Arabelle curtsied to the floor, like Maria. Boris did a low bow with flourishes. The audience roared its approval.

Carried away by the clamorous outpouring, a radiant Arabelle aimed her smiles at the shining faces in the front row. She would remember her friends forever. She would remember this night forever.

Overwhelmed by the applause that greeted her, Deirdre Alexis Glendenning, the toast of London, flung kisses to her adoring public. A rich baritone voice rose above the rest. "Brava! Brava!" The famous actress looked up at the balcony and met the bold eyes of Denys Fitzroy, the Earl of Egmond. The blood-red rose he tossed landed at her feet. She had received many roses before this, but none as beautiful as his.

Mr. Zee shooed the cast back for a final curtain call. Holding hands, they stepped forward, bowed, then stepped back and headed for the wings at a trot. The audience yelled for more and out they went again.

Chip started the chant. "Mr. Zee! Mr. Zee! Mr. Zee!" The audience chanted along, clapping in time.

Chip and Boris dragged Mr. Zee out on stage to take a bow. The audience cheered and stamped and whistled.

"Zackie!" Mrs. Becker waved her program at Mr. Zee. "Zackie, it's Camille! Olga Katrina, the Orpheus Theater, seven curtain calls!"

Mr. Zee grinned and shook his head. "I can't hear," he mouthed at her.

"That's Camille Becker," Arabelle told him. "She used to be a famous actress."

Mr. Zee shouted in disbelief, "Camille?" And with the whole world watching, Walt Zacharias bounded from the stage, swept Mrs. Becker into his arms, and kissed her on both cheeks.

Everyone sat back down to see what was next. Particularly when Mr. Zee got tangled up in Mrs. Becker's feather boa.

Several moments passed before the audience understood that the play was over and what happened between Mr. Zee and Mrs. Becker was not act four. And it was another moment before the stage crew lowered the curtain and brought up the house lights. Mr. Zee and Mrs. Becker, their mouths going a mile a minute, had their arms around each other.

As the crowd headed slowly to the doors, Arabelle jumped off the stage into the arms of her adoring public. Mr. Wexler held out the yellow mums. "Was I all right, Grandpa? Did you like the play? Are you glad you came? You laughed, Mr. Huckabee, I heard you. Thanks for wearing a shirt, Mr. Rosen." It was flesh-colored. No wonder she had worried. "Are you proud of me, Grandpa —" Arabelle paused, startled by how he worked his mouth.

Instead of "help me!" Grandpa Wexler moved his lips in a way she hadn't seen before, his eyes intent on her face. "Are you proud of me, Grandpa?" she asked again. The back of her neck tingled.

"Was I okay?" she said, smiling encouragement. You can do it, her eyes told him. She waited through another struggle and almost missed his whispered "Yes."

"What, Grandpa? I didn't hear." They both knew she had.

"Yes," he said, this time a little louder.

Arabelle threw her arms around him. "Yes! Yes! Yes! The most beautiful word in the whole world."

"Heaven above, what's going on?" Happy cried.

"Mr. Wexler just said 'yes,' didn't you, Grandpa, didn't you?"

"Help me! Help me!"

"Didn't you just say 'yes'?"

Once again his lips moved. Once again Arabelle waited. "Yes," he said after the briefest struggle yet. Never had one word held so much joy or promise.

Happy made Mr. Wexler repeat "yes" for Gwenda and Lana, who had missed it. "Good for you, Wexler." Mr. Rosen thumped him on the back. "About time," Mr. Huckabee grumped.

"I'm so proud of you, Grandpa." Arabelle cradled her mums in one arm and wrapped her other arm around his waist.

"I've just had the best idea," Gwenda said. "Let's read *You Can't Take It With You* Saturday morning, when

Arabelle's with us. We'll divide the parts up."

Happy's eyes sparkled. "Gwenda, you are a treasure."

"I want to be Tony Kirby," Mr. Huckabee said. "Who wants to be Alice?"

Mr. Wexler raised his finger.

"You're too old, Wexler."

"You're kind of old yourself, Huckabee," Mr. Rosen said.

"Don't care what you say," Mr. Huckabee muttered.

"Now, now," Happy chided, "age doesn't matter. We'll toss a coin. That way it'll be fair."

"What's fair about a coin toss?" Mr. Huckabee grumbled. "Clarabelle, you decide."

Arabelle prayed for inspiration. She mustn't disappoint her friends. They cared about her. She cared about them. "Let's take turns reading all the parts," she suggested.

"What a grand idea," Happy said. "Who agrees that Arabelle should be Essie?"

All the hands went up.

"Shall I wear my tutu and dance, Grandpa?"

Mr. Wexler nodded, and out popped "Yes," the word she most wanted to hear. It came faster and easier every time he said it. Tomorrow she'd work with him on a new word — one they'd share forever, like a favorite song.

Mrs. Becker, who had become separated from Mr. Zee, rushed over to Arabelle, her arms outstretched. "You were utterly divine, dahling."

Happy caught Mrs. Becker before she fell. "We've just finished telling her that, Camille. Where in the world is your walker?"

"Fiddledeedee! I told Zackie you should've had seven curtain calls. And those pratfalls! That's what we used to call them — pratfalls. Of course that was before your time. At first we thought you had an accident, didn't we, Mr. Wexler? What a clever minx you are."

"The first one was, Mrs. Becker." No use pretending.

"Well, you fooled us. That's what you should do. Keep the audience guessing. Don't let us see the ace up your sleeve."

"You never told me that you and Mr. Zee were friends, Mrs. Becker."

"I'd no idea 'til I looked at the program. Zackie was Tony Kirby in *You Can't Take It With You*. He was the youngest actor in our touring company, and the handsomest. No one called him Walter. The girls used to line up after every performance. Zackie had the pick of the lot." Mrs. Becker closed her eyes, remembering. "I was a little too old for him back then. In today's world it wouldn't matter a fig."

"What happened?" Arabelle asked. "How come he's teaching high school?"

"One of those girls in line snagged him. Right out from under our noses."

Mr. Huckabee sniggered. "Right out from under your nose, you mean."

"I do not, you old goat. Next thing we knew, Zackie had a wife and baby to support, and no money. He decided to leave the theater. He did the right thing, of course, but it was a great loss."

"He does summer theater, Mrs. Becker. Did he tell you?"

"Of course. I plan to cheer him on from the front row next summer."

Happy was helping Lana button up coats and retrieve fallen gloves. "Is everyone ready?" she called. "We mustn't keep the van waiting."

"Omigosh, are you leaving?"

"Dahling, it's way past our bedtime."

"I should've been asleep hours ago," Mr. Huckabee grumped.

"You can't go yet. I want you to meet my mom and dad. Arabelle rushed over to her parents, who were waiting in the aisle. "Mom, Daddy! Come meet my friends from Heavenly Rest. They're about to leave."

Mrs. Archer held out her arms. "You were terrific, sweetie. Wasn't she terrific, Lyman?"

"Very, very good." Two verys and a good from her father was high praise. He rarely went overboard about anything non-scientific.

Arabelle cast a look at her Heavenly Rest friends. "Mom, Daddy, you mustn't mind what they say," she said under her breath. "Grandpa — Mr. Wexler still says 'help me' once in a while. Mrs. Becker will try to monopolize you. She can't help it, being an actress and all. Daddy, Happy likes to hold your hand so she can pat it. Please, please just let her hold it —"

"Sweetie, don't worry. Your father and I will behave,

won't we, Lyman?"

"We'll do our best."

She didn't stick around after she introduced them. Sometimes it was better not to. She had no worries about her mom, who hit it off with everyone she met. Her father, on the other hand, might scare them to death.

Jeff, Boris, and Erna Sue caught up with her as she headed downstairs to the dressing room.

"Yo, Shorty, hold up."

"You're not going to believe what we just witnessed," Erna Sue said, her face a picture of satisfaction.

"Da! You never guess. Bonnie —"

Jeff clamped his hand over Boris's mouth.

"Seeing is believing, Peanut. Quick, before it's too late." Jeff pulled Arabelle after him as Erna Sue and Boris led the way through the auditorium and up the aisle.

"What's going on?" Arabelle asked.

Motioning for silence, Jeff steered them to a spot in the hallway where they had a perfect view of the lobby. Bonnie Atwood stood in front of the outer doors, facing the departing crowd.

"Hi, everyone! I'm Bonnie Atwood. I played Alice in tonight's show. Are any of you looking for me, by any chance?"

"You were great, Alice. We love ya!"

Bonnie's smile flickered when she saw that the voice belonged to the football coach.

"Excuse me," she called, her smile again on high

beam as another group headed for the doors. "I'm Bonnie Atwood, in case one of you is looking for me. I was Alice Sycamore in the play. Tony's fiancée."

The wraparounds, spouting compliments, stopped to chat her up.

A look of panic crossed Bonnie's face. "I'm sorry, I can't talk. I'm meeting someone." She darted across the lobby, waving to a group by the far door. "Hi! Are you looking for me? I'm Bonnie Atwood."

Jeff and Boris hooted with laughter. Arabelle's grin matched Jeff's. The vision of Bonnie scouring the lobby for an imaginary talent scout was too delicious. How much better a way to get even than ratting her out.

"Justice has been served," Erna Sue said, pumping her arm in victory.

Arabelle had the dressing room to herself. The others had changed and gone to the cast party in the cafeteria. She stood in front of the mirror and gazed at the girl in the shimmering pink tutu and the satin slippers. She wanted to brand Essie Carmichael in her memory forever. She wanted to remember the exact moment when she and Essie became one and the same person, and she wanted to remember when the world laughed and applauded Essie in her darkest hour. On a whim, she raised her leg behind her and held tight to the dressing table. As arabesques went, this one wasn't too bad.

Tomorrow she would be Essie one last time. After that she'd stop being someone she wasn't. Tonight she had banished Maria Tallchief from her life. Deirdre's days, too, were numbered. She would donate her copy of *Ravished!* to the Grafton Green used-book sale.

There was a light knock at the door. "You there, Shorty?"

"Come in, Jeff." She lowered her arms and leg for the last time.

"Hey, I've got something for you." He stood in the doorway, his arms behind his back.

She waited, smiling, unable to guess what it was.

He brought out a long-stemmed red rose. "For Essie Carmichael, who stole the show tonight."

Arabelle burst into tears.

Jeff's face fell. "I thought you'd be pleased."

"I am," she sobbed.

"Then why are you crying?"

"Because it's so beautiful — more beautiful than Denys Fitzroy's rose."

Storm clouds gathered in the dressing room. "Who's Denys Fitzroy? Your boyfriend?"

She hesitated. Should she tell him? What if he made fun of her? She was sure he would. Still . . . "Do you remember Deirdre Glendenning, Jeff? The heroine of *Ravished!*?"

"Yeah, I remember. What about her?"

"Well, in the novel, Deirdre escapes from her cruel master and goes to London where she becomes a famous actress. On a morning ride, she's waylaid by bandits who steal her horse and hang her from a tree. That part isn't in the book. I made it up. Denys Fitzroy, the Earl of Egmond, discovers her in time and cuts her down. I made him up too after you told me your middle name. Egmond is a horse-and-sword man who saves maidens when he's not vanquishing the enemy." She didn't dare look at Jeff.

"Egmond is totally smitten with Deirdre," she went on. "Every night he's in the audience. Whenever she takes a curtain call, he throws a blood-red rose at her feet. Like yours, Jeff, but nowhere near as beautiful." She checked his face.

Jeff Anderson broke up. "What a crazy girl!" he whooped between belly laughs.

She humored him with a smile. "Are you through? It's not that funny."

"You telling me I'm the Earl of Egmond?"

"There are similarities." She said this with a completely straight face.

"Well, if that's the case, I'd better start acting like him." And without any hesitation or hint of what was coming, he pulled her close and kissed her the way Denys Fitzroy would have if he existed, which wasn't the least bit brotherly or brief. This was a serious kiss, with a beginning, a middle, and an end, and the last thing Arabelle expected. She kissed him back the same way, her arms around his neck. Neither of them heard the door open.

"Excuse us! Are we interrupting?" Erna Sue and Boris stood grinning in the doorway.

"Big time," Jeff said. He held Arabelle a second longer, then let her go. She almost wept.

"Erna Sue, why aren't you and Boris at the cast party?"

"We were, Alex. The food's going fast. We thought you should know."

"Mr. Zee say for you to come."

Arabelle sighed. A summons by Mr. Zee trumped Jeff Anderson's arms. "Should I change or can I go this way?"

"You look great, Shorty."

"Da, no change."

"Erna Sue?"

"Go as Essie, Alex. Mr. Zee will be pleased."

"Wait, there is one thing . . ." Arabelle went to the dressing table and shook out her hair, which tumbled in waves to her shoulders. Jeff had never seen her with her hair loose. She tucked his rose behind her ear. "There, now I'm ready."

Satisfied that she had fulfilled her destiny, Arabelle Archer, the former Deirdre Glendenning, sallied forth to the James Madison cafeteria, where her classmates plied her with cake and punch and proclaimed her awesome, and Jeff Anderson, previously the Earl of Egmond, broke every heart except one. "How about it, Shorty? You and me, the winter dance?" To which she replied, "Prithee, Sir Jeffrey, I am pleased to accept." And with her classmates and Mr. Zee looking on, Arabelle twirled on the balls of her feet one last time, in a perfect imitation of herself.